You're About to Become a

*Privileged*

*Woman.*

## INTRODUCING
## *PAGES & PRIVILEGES*™.

It's our way of thanking you for buying
our books at your favorite retail store.

## *GET ALL THIS FREE*

## WITH JUST ONE PROOF OF PURCHASE:

◆ Hotel Discounts up to 60% at home and abroad

◆ Travel Service - Guaranteed lowest published
airfares plus 5% cash back on tickets

◆ $25 Travel Voucher

◆ Sensuous Petite Parfumerie collection ($50 value)

◆ Insider Tips Letter with sneak previews of
upcoming books

◆ Mystery Gift (if you enroll before 6/15/95)

*You'll get a FREE personal card, too.*
*It's your passport to all these benefits– and to*
*even more great gifts & benefits to come!*
*There's no club to join. No purchase commitment. No obligation.*

# As a Privileged Woman,
## you'll be entitled to all these *Free Benefits.*
## And *Free Gifts,* too.

To thank you for buying our books, we've designed an exclusive FREE program called *PAGES & PRIVILEGES™*. You can enroll with just one Proof of Purchase, and get the kind of luxuries that, until now, you could only read about.

## BIG HOTEL DISCOUNTS

**A privileged woman stays in the finest hotels**. And so can you—at up to 60% off! Imagine standing in a hotel check-in line and watching as the guest in front of you pays $150 for the same room that's only costing you $60. Your *Pages & Privileges* discounts are good at Sheraton, Marriott, Best Western, Hyatt and thousands of other fine hotels all over the U.S., Canada and Europe.

## FREE DISCOUNT TRAVEL SERVICE

**A privileged woman is always jetting to romantic places.** When <u>you</u> fly, just make one phone call for the lowest published airfare at time of booking—<u>or double the difference back</u>! PLUS—

you'll get a $25 voucher to use the first time you book a flight AND <u>5% cash back on every ticket you buy thereafter through the travel service</u>!

**Enroll Today in *PAGES & PRIVILEGES*™, the program that gives you Great Gifts and Benefits with just one purchase!**

# *Enrollment Form*

## ☐ *Yes!* I WANT TO BE A *Privileged Woman.*

Enclosed is one *PAGES & PRIVILEGES*™ Proof of Purchase from any Harlequin or Silhouette book currently for sale in stores (Proofs of Purchase are found on the back pages of books) and the store cash register receipt. Please enroll me in *PAGES & PRIVILEGES*™. Send my Welcome Kit and FREE Gifts -- and activate my FREE benefits -- immediately.

NAME (please print)

ADDRESS                                                                          APT. NO

CITY                              STATE                    ZIP/POSTAL CODE

PROOF OF PURCHASE

**NO CLUB!**
**NO COMMITMENT!**
*Just one purchase brings you great* **Free Gifts** *and* **Benefits!**
*(See inside for details.)*

Please allow 6-8 weeks for delivery. Quantities are limited. We reserve the right to substitute items. Enroll before October 31, 1995 and receive one full year of benefits.

Name of store where this book was purchased_____

Date of purchase_____

Type of store:

     ☐ Bookstore   ☐ Supermarket   ☐ Drugstore

     ☐ Dept. or discount store (e.g. K-Mart or Walmart)

     ☐ Other (specify)_____

Which Harlequin or Silhouette series do you usually read?

---

**Complete and mail with one Proof of Purchase and store receipt to:**

  **U.S.:** *PAGES & PRIVILEGES*™, P.O. Box 1960, Danbury, CT 06813-1960

  **Canada:** *PAGES & PRIVILEGES*™, 49-6A The Donway West, P.O. 813, North York, ON M3C 2E8    PRINTED IN U.S.A

# "This is wrong."

"You're supposed to be kissing my fingers," she said unsteadily.

Rui looked at her, then his eyes dropped to her parted lips and down to the impassioned rise and fall of her breasts.

"Fingers are all you're offering?" he enquired.

Sorcha nodded.

"In that case, I'll pass," he said, and strode off to the Jeep.

*ELIZABETH OLDFIELD*'s writing career started as a teenage hobby, when she had articles published. However, on her marriage the creative instinct was diverted into the production of a daughter and son. A decade later, when her husband's job took them to Singapore, she resumed writing and had her first romance accepted in 1982. Now hooked on the genre, she produces an average of three books a year. They live in London, and Elizabeth travels widely to authenticate the background of her books.

## Books by Elizabeth Oldfield

# ELIZABETH OLDFIELD

## Final Surrender

## Harlequin Books

TORONTO • NEW YORK • LONDON
AMSTERDAM • PARIS • SYDNEY • HAMBURG
STOCKHOLM • ATHENS • TOKYO • MILAN
MADRID • WARSAW • BUDAPEST • AUCKLAND

ISBN 0-373-11747-7

FINAL SURRENDER

Copyright © 1992 by Elizabeth Oldfield.

First North American Publication 1995.

This edition published by arrangement with Harlequin Enterprises B.V.

® and TM are trademarks of the publisher. Trademarks indicated with
® are registered in the United States Patent and Trademark Office, the
Canadian Trade Marks Office and in other countries.

Printed in U.S.A.

# CHAPTER ONE

AMONG the ranks of sombrely clad mourners, the girl's scarlet jacket created a vivid and defiant splash of colour. So this was the much-complained-about wild child and family scandal? She was not what he had expected.

As the minister began to intone the words of the burial service and the people around him bowed their heads, Rui undertook a discreet, but thorough inspection. Although he knew she was twenty-five, the impression he had been given was of a sulky nymphet who perpetually stomped around in ripped jeans and bovver boots—yet on the opposite side of the grave stood a chic and adult young woman. With high cheekbones, full mouth and a flawless complexion, she was certainly as pretty as had been claimed, though he would never describe her looks as 'angelic'. Indeed, the contrast of somewhat fierce dark brows with her mane of silver-gold hair hinted at the touch of the devil which had engendered so much mayhem. Rui's eyes fell. Neither could he see anything remotely ethereal about the tempting curves of her body or in the shapely black-

stockinged legs which stretched endlessly down
from a skirt which was no more than a pelmet.

His forehead furrowed. She had often been
bawled out for being a 'selfish, hard-hearted little
bitch', he recalled, but that description jarred
with the visual evidence, too. As she stared down
at the polished mahogany coffin, she struck him
as being unsure, troubled and appealingly vulnerable. Was she regretting what had clearly been
a spectacularly belligerent relationship? Did she
long to turn back the clock and cancel out the
past? Could she be wishing there was some way
in which she could atone for her sins? The gusty
February wind made a grab for his tie and Rui
tucked it firmly back in place. He had scant
patience with those who caused trouble for
others—and in this case the trouble had been
exorbitant and perverse—but, he supposed, a
belated repentance was better than none.

All of a sudden, as though sensing herself
under surveillance, the girl looked up. Wide sea-
green eyes met his, her chin lifted, and she stared
unflinchingly back. Sorcha Riordan did not seem
quite so vulnerable any more.

'I couldn't believe it when I heard your stepfather had dropped down dead in the street,' announced a middle-aged woman whom Sorcha
vaguely recognised as a neighbour, buttonholing
her as she wove her way through the crowd which

filled the large, Persian-carpeted drawing-room. 'He seemed such an athletic fellow.'

'A fitness freak,' she agreed.

After the funeral, her mother had invited everyone back to the family home for a drink and something to eat. In the wide bay window a generous finger buffet was laid out for people to help themselves, but Sorcha and her brother, Michael, had been serving the more elderly seated guests with smoked salmon sandwiches and canapés.

'Denise told me how close the two of you were,' the woman confided, fastening ringed fingers around her arm like a handcuff, 'so I understand your feeling of utter devastation.'

Sorcha gave a silent scream. After suffering the trauma of her first marriage collapsing, her mother had become determined to present a united family front—determined as in obsessed. This meant that the bad blood which existed between Sorcha and her stepfather had been kept a strict secret and, so far as the outside world was concerned, they had revelled in an affectionate affinity. Time and again she had railed against the deception and yet, because her mother cared so much, felt pressured into going along with it.

'I shall miss Jorge,' she replied, thinking that this was true in so much as, when she came here to the spacious stone house on the outskirts of

Southampton, she would miss juggling her visits to try and coincide with his absences.

'By the time they reach their fifties so many men have become fat and flabby, but not him. He kept himself in marvellous shape,' continued the neighbour, in the admiring tones of one who had been smitten. 'And he was such a gentleman. I've never known anyone with such courtly manners, or so attentive.'

'Ladled out charm by the bucketful,' Sorcha said crisply.

All day people, with an accent on the female variety, had been singing paeans of praise, and it was beginning to grate. She recoiled from playing the woebegone stepdaughter—and the fraud. Collecting Brownie badges for telling lies was not her style.

'Yes, Jorge was blessed with charisma,' his fan agreed, oblivious to any sarcasm. 'Why, I remember how once——'

'The minister appears to be in need of a refill,' Sorcha interrupted, with a gesture through the chattering throng, and already moving away. 'I'm supposed to be on hostess duty, so if you'd please excuse me?'

After pouring the clergyman a second sherry and topping up several other glasses, fresh supplies were required. She opened a new bottle in the kitchen and had just returned when, out of the corner of her eye, she noticed the woman eagerly making her way towards her from the far side of the room. Their conversation was to be resumed? She was expected to listen to yet another drooling glorification of Jorge Almeida and make suitably acquiescent noises? Sorcha shuddered. No, thanks. Intent on escape, she spun around, took a hasty step forward and crashed—whump!—into a man who had been approaching from behind. Knocked off balance and wobbling on her high heels, Sorcha raised her hands in an attempt to steady herself—and watched in dismay as droplets of golden liquid spiralled out of the bottle she was carrying to bead the lapel of his immaculate black jacket.

'Sorry,' she said, and lurched forward, meaning to brush the drops away, but as she moved the bottle tipped and what seemed like a veritable river of sherry glugged out to drench his sleeve. 'I'm so sorry,' Sorcha apologised.

'I was warned you have a tendency for going over the top,' her victim remarked, in a smoky, accented voice, 'but I'd decided some of the stories must be exaggerated.' Drolly, he eyed his dripping arm. 'Seems I was wrong. No one can accuse you of not being a whole-hogger.'

Tall, broad-shouldered, and in his mid-thirties, the man possessed the kind of calm self-assurance which friends called confidence and enemies often decried as arrogance. He was also the individual who had been frowning at her in the churchyard.

Sorcha's hackles rose. Old habits died hard and, perhaps as a last statement of revolt, she had chosen to wear a fire-engine-red matador jacket over a dress which, although charcoal-grey, was clingy and rather short. Patterned stockings and suede needle-heeled ankle boots completed her outfit. But, in a three-piece black suit, white shirt and black silk tie, he was classically and appropriately dressed for the occasion. Earlier it had seemed that Mr Dignified disapproved of her appearance and had been berating her for a lack of respect. Her green eyes glittered. She had not appreciated being condemned by a stranger, and now she resented the implication that the spillage was entirely her fault.

Sorcha dispensed a packaged airline smile. 'If you hadn't been so close, we wouldn't have bumped into each other,' she informed him. 'However, if you would care to come with me, I'll sponge your sleeve,' she offered, a mite begrudgingly.

'Thank you, ma'am,' he replied, with a sardonic bow of his head, and dutifully followed her out along the hall.

In the kitchen the man removed his jacket and handed it over, then he leant back against one of the pine units with shirt-sleeved arms negligently folded. As she located a towel to first blot away the excess sherry, Sorcha sneaked him a look from beneath her lashes. Who was he? The accent, plus his thick dark hair and golden skin, identified him as one of the contingent who had flown over from Portugal for the funeral, so he must be either a member of her stepfather's family or one of his friends. Whichever, it placed another black mark against him. A big one.

'Are you an Almeida nephew?' she enquired, deciding that the limitless cool might well be attributed to his having been born with a shiny silver spoon firmly lodged in his well-shaped mouth and that he could number among the copious progeny of her stepfather's three older brothers.

He shook his head. 'My name's Rui de Braganca. I was coming to introduce myself when you pole-axed—when we collided,' he adjusted, with the tilt of a brow. 'I'm the manager of Club Marim.'

'I didn't realise it merited one,' Sorcha said, in blunt surprise.

Several years ago, her stepfather had inherited a substantial acreage of land overlooking the sea on the Algarve. Although most of it consisted of fields left to run wild, on the land were half a dozen villas owned by foreigners who used them as holiday homes, plus a tiny clubhouse with snack bar and swimming-pool. The development, such as it was, had sounded two-bit.

However, Jorge had gone there at regular intervals and she had always assumed that, while topping up his film-star tan would doubtless be a priority, his visits had taken care of whatever overseeing was required.

'You think the place runs itself?' Rui de Braganca demanded, as though speaking to a dimwit. 'How? Not only does the hotel require vast amounts of tender, loving care, but——'

'There's a hotel?' Sorcha broke in.

He nodded. 'It's been in operation for almost two years now. The clubhouse was demolished and a sixty-bedroom hotel with bar and restaurant erected on the site.' A quick, and unexpectedly disarming grin touched the corners of his mouth. 'Despite being so new on the scene, the hotel's already begun to gain a reputation for quality and, given time, could rank among the finest in Portugal. There have been other changes, too.'

'Like what?' she asked, intrigued.

Although it had been impossible to avoid her stepfather completely, on the occasions when he had been around Sorcha had done her best to keep aloof and purposely never shown any interest in his activities—and now gaping holes in her knowledge were becoming apparent.

'As a result of a concerted building programme, the number of villas has been quadrupled, and we operate a management service which looks after them when they're empty and makes sure everything runs smoothly when they're occupied. We also do a brisk trade in renting out the villas on their owners' behalf. The sporting facilities have been extended to include a far larger pool, ten-court tennis complex, and indoor squash and basketball.' The quick grin came again. 'Our latest project is a conference centre which is currently under construction and scheduled to open early next year. You're giving away your dental secrets,' he told her.

'Sorry?' Sorcha said, then realised she had been staring at him in open-mouthed amazement.

Yet to discover that someone whom she had dismissed as little more than a playboy had possessed the imagination and oomph necessary to transform Club Marim into what sounded to be an exceedingly snappy concern *was* amazing. Admittedly the English branch of the Almeida Wine Company, which Jorge had headed, flourished and made a healthy profit, but that had been thanks to an excellent product and dedicated staff, not to him. His brothers might work hard and long at the Lisbon headquarters, yet he had spent more time sailing his yacht on the Solent than at his desk. Sorcha's brow creased. Once before she had seriously misjudged her stepfather, and she had, it seemed, seriously misjudged him again.

'The Algarve enjoys more than three thousand hours of sunshine a year, and as it has its own beach Club Marim is perfect for the sunworshipper,' her companion continued, his hands sketching the air as his enthusiasm gathered and gripped. 'For those who prefer to absorb the local atmosphere, Praia do Marim, a small fishing village, is within easy walking distance, while Lagos, the town from where the great Portuguese discoverers sailed in the fifteenth and sixteenth centuries, is a short drive away. If you're into water sports or big-game fishing we——'

'You've convinced me,' she cut in, impatient of what seemed destined to be a lengthy eulogy. 'Club Marim is a good place for a holiday.'

A muscle tightened in his jaw. 'A *great* place,' he said emphatically.

'It's odd I haven't heard my mother or the twins talk about going there,' Sorcha mused as she wrung out a cloth in cold water.

'That's because they haven't been.' Rui looked beyond her to the garden where the chill wind was buffeting the bare branches of the trees. 'Jorge said he preferred not to mix business with pleasure, so family holidays were spent elsewhere.'

'Like Florida or the Bahamas,' she recalled, thinking of the postcards her mother had sent. 'By the way, I'm Sorcha Riordan, Jorge's stepdaughter,' she added, belatedly and very obviously.

'*A rebelde,*' he remarked.

'Sorry?'

'You're the *enfant terrible* who niggled the hell out of the poor guy,' Rui said, in a matter-of-fact, if somewhat biting translation.

Sorcha shot him a startled look. Her mother's need for public perfection meant that, in addition to her and Jorge's warring being kept under wraps, a blanket of silence had been thrown over the crimes and misdemeanours which she had committed down the years. With enormous pretence, Sorcha had been ceaselessly depicted as the respectable, well-behaved and obedient offspring. A round-the-clock Girl Guide. She had believed her stepfather to be one hundred per cent loyal to the charade, but the *enfant terrible* tag and, now that she remembered it, his talk of her going over the top, indicated that Rui de Braganca had been granted access to a certain amount of information.

'Jorge spoke about—about me?' Sorcha faltered as she began to dab at the jacket.

'Whenever he was at Club Marim. But don't worry, I'm the only one he unburdened himself to, and I've realised you're an alabaster virgin,' Rui said, his tone dry, 'and that everything between the two of you was supposed to have been sweetness and light.'

She gave a synthetic smile. 'What did he say?' she enquired.

'That you were a tearaway.'

'He provided examples?'

'Yes.'

'Such as?' Sorcha demanded.

Rui rubbed a reflective fingertip slowly back and forth across his lower lip. 'Jorge told me how, a year or so after he married your mother, you got yourself expelled from school.'

'When I was thirteen. And?' she prodded.

'How you'd then insisted on joining your brother at his boarding-school, but were soon hauled before the headmaster and almost expelled again.'

'For smoking.'

'I believe it was considered to be a crime of the utmost depravity,' he said, and his brown eyes sparkled.

While there was no question but that much of her behaviour had been reprehensible, there were occasions when Rui had found her so-called vices innocuous, if not downright amusing. Jorge's censure might have been relentless, but memories of Rui's own youthful wayward streak meant he understood and was inclined to sympathise.

'You believe right,' Sorcha replied stiffly. 'Do continue, Mr de Braganca.'

'Rui,' he said.

'Do continue, Rui.'

'Jorge talked about how, if you were forbidden to go to a party, you'd wait until everyone was asleep then climb out of the bathroom window. And about the time you slipped on his boat, and, not by accident, or so he claimed, knocked him into the water, fully dressed and right outside the yacht club.' As he recalled the narrator's almost comic outrage at this embarrassment his mouth curved. 'And other similar incidents.'

Sorcha rubbed savagely at the sleeve. So her stepfather, the creep, had gone in for family revelations in a big way. How dared he? Despite the oft-repeated insistence that she would welcome it if everyone would please be honest, she felt double-crossed and furious. She objected to being discussed behind her back. She begrudged Rui de Braganca's being treated to an unauthorised account of her escapades. Her personal history was *hers*, dammit! She also resented being viewed as a figure of fun.

'As well as Jorge's employee, you appear to have been his confidant,' she said, her tone sharp with accusation.

Rui's expression sobered. 'I guess he used me as a shoulder to cry on because he felt we had something in common.'

'You also have a stepdaughter whom you endlessly criticise?' Sorcha demanded scathingly.

'No. I'm single.' He hesitated. 'Look, I'm sorry if you're upset, but——'

'I'm not.'

'In that case, could you go a little easier on my jacket?' Rui appealed. 'I'd prefer it if I didn't leave here with a sleeve full of holes.'

Sorcha controlled her rubbing. 'How come you speak such good English?' she asked, for, although he had the kind of attractively intruiging accent which actors would spend years perfecting, he was completely at ease in the language.

'My parents felt it essential their children should be fluent, so I had private lessons when I was young, but also I've spent some time in the States. You aren't the first daughter to have idolised her father and taken it hard when her mother remarried,' he went on. 'OK, so you regarded Jorge as an intruder and hit back—with a vengeance. It was regrettable, but what's done is done and feeling guilty now won't change——'

Something inside Sorcha pinched and twisted. 'Guilty?' she repeated.

'At the graveside you seemed pensive, as though you were——'

'It didn't occur to you that I might have been debating whether or not to give a resounding three cheers?' she demanded.

'No, though I don't doubt it would have put a kick into the proceedings,' he remarked, in stern reproof.

Sorcha drew in a breath. Bereavement was said to come at the top of life's stress scale, and whatever her feelings for her stepfather—*because* of those feelings—all day a tension had been growing inside her. But now, with her talk of hip-hip-hoorahs, she was being truculent and behaving badly. It was an unwelcome reversion to the past.

'Although I admit there was a time when I longed for some gruesome fate to befall Jorge, I didn't want him to die,' she said, her tone calmer. 'He was kind to my mother and a loving father to the twins. He also got on well with Michael. All of them will mourn him and feel his loss, and so I'm sorry. That he and I didn't hit it off was——' a shadow crossed her face '—just one of those things. However,' Sorcha could not resist finishing, 'I'd like to point out that, whatever stories you've heard, you only heard Jorge's version—and he emitted a lot of hot air.'

'So, when you worked for the kissogram agency, you didn't specialise in "naughty nuns"?' Rui enquired, with an amused twitch of his lips.

She sighed impatiently. 'Yes, I did.'

'How about being a punk?'

'I wore a lot of black eye make-up at one period, if that's what you mean.'

His grin widened. 'They say you should try everything, except tiger wrestling and homicide.'

'You should have tried handling my step-father's aggression!' Sorcha retorted. 'He found faults where there weren't any and repeatedly accused me of doing things I hadn't done and would never do, like taking drugs. He was also stuck in a time-warp and insisted on forever regarding me as a naughty teenager. Despite all the evidence, he refused to accept I'd grown up or that I'd stopped misbehaving.'

Rui gave her a speculative frown. 'You're a reformed character?' he enquired.

'Have been for years—and for years I've been prepared to live and let live, but Jorge wasn't responsive. Whenever we met he'd rant and rave about something—either my living in London, or my friends, or when I intended to stop "dabbling", as he called it. He was so bloody interfering, and he had absolutely no sense of humour. But the worst thing was his insistence that it was *my* fault we were enemies. I'm not saying I'm entirely——' Sorcha stopped dead. Her personal motto had always been 'never explain, never complain', so why was she jabbering on like this now? Jabbering tempestuously. Dangerously. Jabbering to someone she had not even met until a quarter of an hour ago. 'The cuff's damp but it's wearable,' she said, thrusting his jacket back at him, 'and I must make the tea.'

Rui pushed a long arm halfway into a sleeve. 'I'm safe? You're not planning to pour the pot over me?' he enquired laconically.

'I shall keep well away,' she assured him.

Far away, Sorcha resolved as she filled cups and offered plates of fruitcake and biscuits to the guests. Her stepfather's demise meant the past could also be buried, for once and for all, and she had no wish to wander down memory lane again. None. She looked across to where Club Marim's manager was now in conversation with another of the visitors. What had made her so garrulous with him? she wondered. Apart from her aversion to soul-baring, he was not the kind of man to whom she usually responded. He was too disturbingly masculine. Indeed, with a jaw which looked as though it would gather a five o'clock shadow if he did not shave twice daily, Rui de Braganca was a darkly macho brute. How she could have mistaken him for one of her stepfather's relatives she did not know. The male Almeidas were short, wiry, nimble characters, whereas he must be around six foot three, was well-built, and moved with the easy grace of a big cat. A golden leopard, she decided. Her study of him continued. With a square jaw and granite-hard features, he was arresting rather than handsome, but he possessed an undeniable sex appeal which must have the women falling at his feet like autumn leaves. Sorcha bit into a biscuit.

The sooner Rui de Braganca was back in Portugal, the better.

Half an hour later, when the first guests began to leave, Sorcha decided she would make an exit, too. She had had enough of playing the phoney, and of feeling ill-at-ease. Her injudicious outburst had opened the lid on thoughts which had been resolutely locked away, but which were now leaping up and down in her head like manic jacks-in-the-box. They were thoughts which resurrected feelings of hurt and isolation and...shame.

She spoke to Michael, then went over to say goodbye to her mother. 'How are you feeling?' she asked, her eyes moving anxiously over the slender, still beautiful woman.

Denise Almeida tucked a wisp of hair back into her blonde chignon and smiled. 'I'm surviving.'

'Mike'll stay with you until Friday morning and I'll return in the afternoon for the weekend,' Sorcha said, 'as we planned. But I'll phone this evening when I get back to London, and every day,' she added, eager to demonstrate her desire to give all possible support.

She received a warm hug. 'Thank you, darling.'

'If you don't mind, I'll be off now. I've had a word with Mike and he's promised to help with the clearing up. And there's a train at——'

'You can't leave yet,' her mother interrupted. 'Not until we've had the meeting with Mr Dyas.'

'Who's Mr Dyas?' Sorcha asked.

'The solicitor. He's due in forty-five minutes or so. Didn't I tell you how he's coming to talk about Jorge's finances?'

She shook her head. 'Mike didn't mention it, so you can't have told him, either.'

'Oh, dear. I meant to and I was sure I had, but——' Denise Almeida fussed with a pearl earring '—right now I'm not thinking too clearly. You have to be here,' she insisted. 'You need to know what's happening.'

Did she? For Sorcha, all that mattered was that her mother should be able to continue her present lifestyle and educate her seven-year-old twin sons without hardship, and there was no doubt Jorge Almeida would have left his widow exceptionally well-off. She gave a mental shrug. Listening to a recital of stocks, bonds and other investments held no interest, but, if her mother wanted her to sit in, so be it.

'Hello, my pets,' Denise Almeida said as two small boys in white shirts and grey shorts appeared beside them. She ruffled their curly brown hair. 'You are being good.'

'Good enough to have some more ice-cream?' appealed Edward, the older twin.

'The toffee fudge kind?' Sebastian, the younger one, enquired hopefully.

Sorcha gave a mock groan of horror. 'You're not still hungry?' she protested, and her half-brothers giggled.

'Can we, Mum?' Edward pleaded.

Denise Almeida hesitated. They had already had two bowlfuls. 'Tiny helpings,' she agreed, unable to resist them anything today.

'I shall be your servant, sirs,' Sorcha said and, giving a salute which made the twins giggle again, she led the way to the kitchen.

A great-aunt with a penchant for helping had begun to retrieve some of the used glasses and crockery, so, after providing the ice-cream, Sorcha became busy stacking the dishwasher and washing the crystal. By remaining out of the way, she intended to avoid both Rui de Braganca and the Jorge-besotted neighbour. Time passed. The twins went off to the den to watch television, various relatives appeared to bid her farewell, and when the great-aunt brought in her final tray she reported that, as all the guests had gone, she was going, too. Club Marim's manager had departed without bothering to say goodbye? Although it did not make sense, Sorcha felt strangely disappointed.

There were left-over sausage rolls to cling-wrap, wedges of cheese to go in the fridge, biscuits and cakes to be stored in tins. She had just finished putting everything away when a clean-cut young man whose blond good looks echoed her own came in.

'So much for your promise to help,' Sorcha chided.

Her brother gave a sheepish smile. 'Sorry. I've come to tell you Mr Dyas is in the study and ready to start.'

As she went with Michael into the comfortable room with its mullioned windows and honey-coloured panelling Sorcha did a double-take. She had assumed the meeting to be for family only, but Rui de Braganca was sat in one of the leather wing-chairs before the desk. His long legs stretched out, he was chatting amiably with her mother. Irritation stabbed. What was he doing here? As her past had been none of his business, she did not see how her mother's financial status concerned him, either. Holding her head high, she stalked past and took a seat. The manner in which she had babbled indicated that the tall Portuguese had a flair for making friends and influencing people, but surely her mother did not intend to follow Jorge's example and install him as her confidant, too?

Mr Dyas, a thin, sharp-faced, busy man, of-ficiously cleared his throat and, having made sure of his audience's attention, began to speak.

'I intend to read straight through Mr Almeida's last will and testament, and explain the fine print later,' he declared, looking at everyone over the top of his bifocals. 'So, whatever questions you may have, I'd be grateful if you would keep them until the end.'

Sorcha stared at the solicitor in bewilderment. When her mother had spoken of a talk about finances, she had not visualised it to be a formal declaration of the monies Jorge had left.

'The will?' she queried.

'Naturally,' he said, and, adjusting his spectacles, he began to read.

As anticipated, it transpired that her mother was to inherit the bulk of her late husband's estate—which included a quarter holding in his family's wine business. Trust funds were to be established for his young sons, and Michael was to receive a healthy bundle of equities.

'Thank you, Jorge,' he muttered in a delighted undertone.

'"To my stepdaughter——"' Mr Dyas went on.

Sorcha sat bolt upright. 'Me?' she protested, her green eyes stretched wide. 'He's left something to me?'

Displeased by this second interruption, the solicitor frowned. '"To my stepdaughter, Sorcha Riordan, I bequeath fifty-one per cent of the shares in Club Marim,"' he continued, in an irritated staccato. '"And to Rui de Braganca are bequeathed the remaining forty-nine per cent."'

As her mind grappled to contain this bombshell of information, Sorcha swung a sideways look at the club's manager. Like her, he appeared to be in shock—though, in his case, the shock had tensed his body and given a tight intensity to his mouth.

'"To my cousin Fernanda,"' Mr Dyas went on hastily, as though fearful she might disrupt the proceedings again, '"I leave..."' A number of small gifts which the deceased had made to various other relatives and friends were listed, then the solicitor announced that the reading of the will was complete. He nodded at Sorcha. 'Now,' he said, 'you have a query?'

There had to be a million, yet she could not think of one. 'To my stepdaughter...I bequeath...' The words echoed in the thickness of her mind like sounds in a fog. Not for one moment had she thought that she might be a recipient of Jorge's largesse.

'Er—no, no,' Sorcha mumbled, and the solicitor gave an exasperated click of his tongue.

'Could you explain how the twins' trust funds will operate?' Denise Almeida appealed.

Lengthy details were supplied, and a quarter of an hour elapsed before Mr Dyas turned his attention to Club Marim. Even so, Sorcha continued to flounder. The club, she dimly absorbed, was a registered company, and she and Rui de Braganca would take their place on the board as directors and co-owners. As soon as the paperwork had been completed, a visit to Portugal would be necessary in order for her formally to accept the position and put her name to various documents.

'The solicitors over there will acquaint you with the legalities involved,' Mr Dyas informed her, then placed his spectacles back into their case and gathered up his papers. The meeting was over.

'Why on earth should Jorge leave you *anything*?' Michael demanded as their mother ushered the solicitor out to the front door.

Sorcha consciously loosened hands which she realised had been gripped tight. 'Maybe he felt that as you and the twins were to benefit it was only fair I should, too,' she said, her voice throwaway and light.

'But whenever you met it was like a world war!' her brother protested.

He had welcomed their stepfather as a member of the household and complied with his wishes, so it rankled that the troublemaker *extraordinaire* should receive an equal—if not a superior—inheritance.

'Jorge always started any arguments,' she replied.

'That's your story, but the point is he considered you to be a complete pain in the——'

'Jorge had a soft spot for Sorcha,' Denise Almeida vowed, flustered to return and find her children rattling family skeletons in the presence of an outsider. She flashed Rui an embarrassed smile. 'Deep down.'

'Must have been subterranean,' Michael muttered.

Rui rose to his feet. 'How soon will you be able to come out to Portugal?' he asked Sorcha.

She hesitated. 'I'm busy right now, but——'

'Busy starving in a garret?' her brother gibed.

After a trying and tiring day, Sorcha's temper snapped. 'You remind me of Jorge at times, you know that?' she demanded. 'Like he did, you ignore the——'

'I'm sure Rui would like a cup of coffee before he leaves,' Denise Almeida cut in, hastily acting the peacemaker. 'Michael, would you see to the percolator while I check on the twins?'

'When can you visit Portugal?' Rui asked again, the moment they were alone.

Sorcha pursed her lips. 'Not for two months, at least.'

'That long?' he protested.

'I'm afraid so.'

He flexed his shoulders. 'Being given a share in a holiday development might seem like fun and games, but it's essential everything is put on a proper legal footing as soon as possible,' he told her briskly.

'I appreciate that,' she replied. 'However——'

'So when can you come?' Rui demanded.

Sorcha frowned, thinking. 'I could probably manage a few days towards the end of April.'

'Dates?' he demanded, taking a black leather diary from the inside pocket of his jacket.

She blinked. 'No idea.'

He leafed through. 'The twentieth? That's a Monday. It's make-your-mind-up time,' Rui told her sternly.

'Suppose I travel out on Tuesday the twenty-first and stay until the Friday?' Sorcha suggested.

'A room will be reserved and I'll send you an air ticket.' He snapped the diary shut. 'I'd be grateful if you would co-operate by sticking to that arrangement.'

She looked at him. Earlier, while he might not have been entirely approving, he had seemed content to regard her as some kind of vaudeville act, but his attitude had changed. Now that she was to be involved in his world she had become bad news, and a liability. Once condemned, always condemned, Sorcha thought, caught somewhere between anger and exasperation. What else was new?

'You can't have been paying attention earlier,' she said.

'Excuse me?'

She dispensed a thin smile. 'If you'd care to cast your mind back, you'll recall I told you that I no longer make it an absolute rule to foul up everything.'

'You'd better not foul up Club Marim,' he replied, his voice warning and chill. Rui walked to the window, his hands thrust into his trouser pockets and his jacket flaring back. For a minute or two he gazed out, then he turned. 'You and I may have to get into bed together,' he began harshly, 'but——'

Sorcha tossed her hair from her shoulders. 'Don't worry, *I* shan't be the one kicking beneath the sheets,' she announced, and marched from the room.

## CHAPTER TWO

PUSHING her sunglasses on to the top of her head, Sorcha gazed out through the windscreen. The light in the Algarve was different. The air possessed a luminosity which made the cerulean blue of the sky seem deeper, caused the blossoms in the trees to shine a more dazzling white, gave the ochre-red earth a richer hue. Water-colour would be the medium in which to paint the landscape, she decided, but how did you capture the sparkle?

As arranged, the Club Marim minibus had collected her, together with two German couples, from Faro Airport, and for more than an hour they had been driving westwards. Through bustling towns and lazy villages sleeping in the afternoon sun they had sped, past orange groves thick with fruit, and fields of fig and vine, and roadside *artesanato* shops with their racks of gaudily patterned plates and blue and white tiles. Sorcha slid her glasses back on to her nose. It would be interesting to visit a pottery, and she also hoped to find time to relax and maybe start on a tan.

'We are almost there?' one of the German women enquired as the minibus swung off the dual carriageway and on to a quieter, windy, far more rural road.

'In ten minutes,' confirmed Manuel, the driver.

Sorcha's stomach fluttered. Pressure of work meant that this far she had only been able to give her inheritance fleeting and intermittent thought, but now excitement was bubbling—laced with apprehension. She was eager to see Club Marim; what she did not feel so sure about was meeting up with Rui de Braganca again. Did he still believe he had been saddled with a juvenile delinquent? Would he be hostile? Together with the air ticket, he had sent her a copy of Club Marim's brochure and a covering letter; but it had been impossible to read between the brief, typewritten lines. Sorcha crossed mental fingers. She very much hoped that her fellow-director had reconsidered and they could establish an amicable working relationship.

Passing a sign which read 'Praia do Marim', the minibus entered a tight-packed cluster of whitewashed houses. If only she had brought along her sketch-pad, she thought, wistfully eyeing the quaint wooden-shuttered windows and lacy chimney-pots. Already she had seen so much which she itched to record in her clean, spare style. Before too long she would come again, Sorcha resolved, and add some Algarve paintings to her portfolio.

As the road delved between the houses it narrowed and plunged steeply down. A series of jolting bumps across pot-holes, a swerve to avoid an ambling group of tourists, and they reached the square which formed the focus of the tiny community. One glimpse of the harbour with its bobbing, brightly painted boats, and they were off around a corner and charging uphill.

'Here you have best view of Club Marim,' Manuel, a jovial, swarthy man, told them, screeching to a halt at the top in what was a blatant party trick.

'Wow!' one of the Germans obligingly exclaimed from behind her.

'Fabulous, *ja*?' said his wife, and the other couple hastened to agree. The woman, a chatterbox who was not satisfied unless she had drawn everyone into her conversation, patted Sorcha on the shoulder. 'You like it also?'

She turned to grin. 'Very much.'

Wanting to learn more about her bequest, Sorcha had questioned her mother—who had begun by saying that as soon as Jorge had recognised the wealth of opportunities which Club Marim had offered he had gone full speed ahead to bring them to fruition.

'He was never particularly business-minded here,' Denise Almeida had reflected, 'but the development seemed to fire his imagination. I assume its being in his homeland made all the difference.'

'What is Club Marim like?' Sorcha had enquired.

'Don't know. Jorge did talk about it, but I wasn't interested and I've forgotten,' her mother had said offhandedly, and had disappeared to call the twins in from the garden for lunch.

Frustrated at not being able to summon up some kind of a picture, Sorcha had been delighted when the brochure had arrived. It had contained shots of a low sprawling hotel set amid trim lawns, of bougainvillaea-decorated villas, of soft golden sand in the private bay. Narrow-eyed, she now examined the view. The photographs had been a tempting advertisement of the club's desirability, yet they had failed to convey the rolling contours and the spaciousness.

Below and beyond, a wide valley sloped down to the sea, backed in the distance by acres of lush green land. On the slopes of the valley red-roofed houses built in the traditional Moorish style could be glimpsed, discreetly sited among eucalyptus and pine, while in its cleft lay the gleaming white hotel and, off to one side, tennis courts. The combination of nature and man's endeavours had created an environment which was elegant, cared-for and refined. Sorcha swallowed hard. And half of this belonged to her!

After proudly accepting compliments from the Germans, Manuel released the brake. Down the minibus careered, through tall wrought-iron gates and along leafy lanes until, a few minutes later, they reached the porticoed entrance of the hotel. As everyone gathered up their belongings and began clambering out, glass doors slid aside and a tall brunette in a pin-striped navy dress emerged.

'Senhorita Riordan?' she enquired, her dark eyes cool and assessing.

Sorcha removed her sunglasses. 'That's right,' she said with a smile, and felt a flicker of dismay when the girl did not smile back.

It had been obvious Manuel had had no idea that the young woman sitting beside him could lay claim to being his new boss, but the girl did and was wary. Were other members of Club Marim's staff going to be wary of her, too? she wondered. It was an unforeseen complication.

'Senhor de Braganca had planned to greet you on your arrival, but there has been an emergency,' the brunette stated in precise English. She gestured into the marble-floored lobby with its chandeliers and eau-de-Nil sofas. 'If you would care to wait, *senhorita*, I shall——'

'OK, Izabel, *eu acabei de chegar*,' a voice called, and as the girl nodded an acknowledgement and turned her attention to the Germans— she smiled at them—Sorcha swivelled to see a jeep nosing its way into a porch-side parking space and Rui de Braganca vaulting out.

She gazed at him in surprise. Because he had been so conventionally dressed at the funeral she had imagined him wearing a business suit, but he was casual in a short-sleeved button-down denim shirt and jeans. He looked younger than she remembered and, with bare arms and his legs encased in tight-fitting Levis, even more aggressively male.

Sorcha offered a tentative smile. 'Hello,' she said.

'Good afternoon,' he replied, and gave her a strong firm handshake in the customary Portuguese greeting. 'Did you have a good flight?'

'Yes, thanks.'

As he proceeded to make polite enquiries about how she had enjoyed the drive from the airport and her first impressions of Portugal, Sorcha's antennae quivered. Her spirits sank. Her co-director might be going through all the motions of civility, but beneath it could be discerned an aloofness, an asperity, an impatience at her presence. Although not openly hostile, it was clear he had not changed his mind and her credit rating remained at zero.

After giving instructions to Manuel to deliver her luggage to her room Rui shepherded her through the sliding glass doors and across the entrance hall. Opening a door marked 'PRIVATE', he took her along a wide corridor which had offices off on either side.

'I had no idea how you wanted to play things,' he said, as he showed her into an airy, pale-carpeted room which overlooked gardens, 'so, although the staff here have been informed that Jorge left the club to his stepdaughter and to me, only three people are aware Sorcha Riordan *is* his stepdaughter. The three are José, the accountant; Antonio, our resident architect; and——'

'Izabel,' she said.

He looked curious. 'How did you know?'

'Because when we met she kept me at barge-pole distance and seemed critical.' Like you, Sorcha inserted silently. 'Perhaps she resents a woman who's around her own age being in a position of authority here,' she suggested.

Standing with long-fingered hands spread on his lean hips and legs set apart, Rui's eyes travelled over her in a leisurely assessment. 'I'd say it's your outfit Izabel resents,' he replied.

'My outfit?' she queried, with a surprised downwards glance at her cropped black turtle-necked top and matching leggings.

'Like many Portuguese, Izabel tends to be conservative and although she might well love to wear what you're wearing she'd never have the courage to bare her midriff.' Eyes of treacle-toffee-brown met hers in a level look. 'Nor to dispense with her bra.'

Sorcha bridled. When dressing that morning she had pulled on clothes which had seemed easy for the journey—and covered them with an over-sized sweater, now shed—but beneath his gaze what had been purely practical had become pro-vocative. Rui made her aware of how the soft material clung to her breasts and the snug fit of the leggings around her thighs. He also made her feel like a bimbo—which, she thought furiously, might well have been his intention.

'I'm sorry you don't approve,' she replied glacially, 'though I suppose it's to be expected. You didn't approve of what I wore at the fu-neral, either.'

'You've got me wrong,' he said. 'I thought you looked most appealing then, and I do today.'

Sorcha cast him a dubious look. 'Yes?' she said cautiously.

'Especially when you're standing like that.'

In defiance, she had squared her shoulders and thrust out her chest, but now she longed to crumple and shield herself from his gaze. Hot colour seeped under her skin. If Rui de Braganca was in the business of totting up points, he had just scored another one. Damn him!

'What function does Izabel perform here?' Sorcha demanded, desperate to change the subject.

'She's my personal assistant. We work very closely together.' He gestured for her to be seated, then dropped down in the swivel chair behind his desk. 'I need to know whether or not you'd like me to assemble everyone and introduce you.'

Sorcha visualised herself facing rows of laser-eyed strangers, each one as disdainful as him. 'No, thank you,' she replied. 'Until I've got my bearings I'd prefer to be incognito, as far as is possible.'

'Fine. Two appointments have been scheduled for tomorrow,' Rui continued, becoming brisk and businesslike. 'In the morning I've arranged a get-together with José and Antonio, and after lunch we're to have a session with the lawyers. On Thursday morning I'll drive you around the development, and in the afternoon I intend to explain the plans which have been formulated for Club Marim's future.'

'Sounds like a busy two days,' she commented.

A brow lifted. 'You didn't imagine you were coming here to sunbathe?'

'Of course not,' Sorcha replied, with a laugh that was meant to imply the idea was ridiculous.

Sitting back in his chair, Rui rested one foot across the other thigh in autocratic ease. 'I'd like to suggest that José and Antonio are brought on to the board as non-shareholding directors,' he said. 'Each has contributed significantly to the club's success, and the increased status will be both a reward and an encouragement for them to remain. And, as they're high-calibre guys, I'm eager they should remain. It'd be appropriate if they both received a salary increase at the same time, too.'

'How much of an increase?' Sorcha enquired.

Her question seemed to take him by surprise. 'I thought I'd add fifteen per cent.'

'You thought *we'd* add fifteen per cent,' she corrected sweetly.

His lean features tightened. 'I guess.'

'It's you, the big chief, and me, the little Indian?' Sorcha enquired.

Rui might have said that bringing José and Antonio on to the board was a suggestion, yet, in reality, he had been telling her what he had already decided was going to happen. But she had not come all this way to be talked at and talked over in such a cavalier fashion.

'I beg your pardon?' he said.

'Correct me if I'm wrong, but I get the impression you intend our partnership to be run on *your* terms, which means you call the shots while my function is to agree, follow, submit? Sorry, but I do hold shares in Club Marim—the *majority* of them,' she said. Where point-scoring was concerned, Sorcha now considered they were even. 'I agree to José and Antonio coming on to the board,' she told him, with a gracious grand-duchess incline of her head, 'and I also sanction fifteen per cent.'

'Correct me if I'm wrong,' Rui countered, 'but both those decisions are based on total ignorance.'

She glared. 'Well...yes,' she was forced to agree.

Planting both feet on the floor, he sat forward. 'How much time are you intending to spend in Portugal in the future?' he enquired, as though she were a carrier of the Black Death.

Sorcha had visualised spending the minimum, but she was not about to tell him that now. Let him worry. Let him sweat. Let that calm self-assurance be ruffled.

'I haven't decided. However, I shan't be needing an office.' She paused. 'Not yet.'

'An office?' Rui repeated, with ill-concealed horror.

Her eyes travelled oh, so slowly around the room with its teak desk, oval table, bank of sleek grey filing cabinets. 'I wouldn't expect you to give up yours,' Sorcha told him silkily. 'It'll be interesting to take a look around and see whether there are any alterations which I feel ought to be made,' she continued. 'I'll also be able to start formulating *my* plans for Club Marim's future. Look, I'm sorry if my becoming a director here has upset you,' she said, suddenly growing weary of trying to score points, 'but you'll just have to accept that that's the way the mop flops.'

'You mean what can't be cured must be endured?' Rui enquired.

'I mean being in business with me does not equal unmitigated disaster!' Sorcha replied.

He raked her with a disbelieving look, then sat back in his chair and folded his arms. He had muscular arms covered with brown hair which formed a coarse dark lace against the smooth gold of his skin. Was he hairy all over? Sorcha mused in the silence which followed. Her eyes went to the open throat of his shirt. There were no curls of hair to be seen there, but that did not mean——

'Today is my parents' fiftieth wedding anniversary and this evening there's a family celebration,' Rui said, 'so——'

Sorcha jolted back to life. 'Excuse me?' she said, and pinkened, wondering why on earth his bodily hair should be of the remotest interest to her.

'So I'm unable to join you for dinner. However, Antonio——'

'If you don't mind, I'd rather be on my own. I'd like time to unwind.' She hesitated. 'Did my stepfather ever say he intended to leave part of Club Marim to me?' she enquired.

Although Jorge would not have revealed everything—no chance—he had clearly talked at length with his manager, and she was curious to know what reason, if any, had been given for her inheritance.

Rui shook his head. 'He never mentioned his will, but then he wouldn't have imagined he was destined to die so young.'

'And until the solicitor read out the bequests you didn't imagine you'd be a recipient either,' she said, remembering how stunned he had looked.

'On the contrary, it seemed likely.' His lips curved in a fleeting grin. 'Boy, did anyone ever give me what I wanted.'

Sorcha frowned. 'You thought you were in line for some shares?' she queried.

'Yes, though not until the day of the funeral when your mother asked me to stay to meet the solicitor. Then I realised Jorge must have included me in his will, and shares in Club Marim were the obvious thing.'

'But you seemed so shocked,' she protested. 'You were shocked because *I* was the major shareholder!' she said in abrupt realisation and chagrin.

'You betcha,' Rui replied coolly.

Indignation simmered. 'I may be the cloud in your silver lining, but you should be damned grateful I exist,' Sorcha told him.

'Why?' he enquired.

'Because Jorge left you your shares in appreciation of the many hours when you sat flap-eared while he dished the dirt on me!'

'You think I wanted to listen to his ramblings?' Rui demanded.

'I think you needn't have done,' she said crossly, her resentment at having been discussed once again bubbling to the surface. 'I think you could have changed the subject.'

'I tried, but the guy seemed to have a compulsion. However, my bequest had nothing to do with that.' Leaning back again, Rui linked his hands behind his head. 'It was in appreciation of the blood, sweat and tears I've expended turning Club Marim from a one-horse saloon into a viable and thriving concern.'

'You? You're responsible?' Sorcha said in bewilderment. 'But surely my stepfather——?'

'The original idea of building the hotel was mine, plus the tennis centre and all the other improvements. I also supervised everything from start to finish.' He looked at her across the desk. 'You believed Jorge was the one who'd made it happen?'

'Yes. You see...' Sorcha's voice petered away. When her mother had spoken of her stepfather's imagination being fired because the development was in Portugal she had accepted it—despite knowing him to be mentally languid and notoriously work-shy. But Rui brimmed with force,

energy, a keen intelligence. 'Jorge must have
claimed all the glory when he told my mother
about the place,' she said.

'He claimed the glory when he spoke to people
here, too,' Rui remarked, and shrugged.

'It didn't bother you?'

He shook his head. 'Being lauded as the mas-
termind doesn't turn me on; all that matters is
the personal satisfaction of creating one of the
finest holiday developments on the Algarve.'
Suddenly he frowned. 'Jorge hadn't even been
buried before the manager of the bank down in
Praia do Marim was on the phone to say he had
an anonymous client who wanted to buy the
place. I explained I didn't know what'd be happening, and it seems that when the client
eventually learned the development wasn't for
sale he was very disappointed. I received my
shares because I damned well deserved them, but
what did you ever do to deserve yours?' Rui demanded in an abrupt veer.

Sorcha frowned down at her hands. 'I was
Jorge's stepdaughter,' she began carefully,
'and——'

'And that's supposed to be reason enough?
Come on,' he jeered. Impatiently he raked back
strands of dark hair from his brow. 'You have
no knowledge of Portugal, of the leisure industry, nor do you have any business training.'

Her chin lifted. 'So?'

'So the idea of your being a working director and making a worthwhile contribution to Club Marim is downright hilarious. Ripping off a nun's habit and smothering strange men with kisses may demand a certain talent,' Rui mocked, 'but it sure as hell isn't much use when it comes to——' He broke off as the telephone on the desk rang. 'Excuse me,' he said, reaching across to answer it.

He listened to what the caller had to say, then started into what sounded like remonstrances in curt Portuguese. Sorcha waited for a minute or two, but when the conversation showed no sign of ending she rose to her feet. She had had enough of being belittled and disparaged and, if she hurried, maybe she could manage a session beside the pool before the sun set.

'What time is the meeting in the morning?' she asked as he covered the mouthpiece with a large hand.

'Nine-thirty.'

'Here?'

'Here,' Rui confirmed.

Sorcha gave a tight smile. 'I'll see you then.'

It was late afternoon and Sorcha's brain seemed to be in imminent danger of seizing up. She had never realised becoming a company director would mean there was so much to listen to, so much to remember, so much to understand—or try to. The morning had demanded three hours of non-stop concentration. First the architect had insisted on relating a virtual brick-by-brick account of the revamping of Club Marim, then José, a solemn young man, had proceeded to give her what had amounted to a crash course in finance. Working his way through endless balance sheets, he had waxed lyrical on profit margins, sermonised on tax situations, described in detail how the amount of dividend which she and Rui would receive was calculated. At first Sorcha had valiantly kept track, but with his sums and complicated explanations ultimately he had lost her. And now she was at the receiving end of a lecture on Portuguese company law!

On the other side of the table sat two bigwigs from the firm which was handling the ownership transfer. They were cheerful, kindly men, but both used excessive legal jargon and both were long-winded. That their English was fractured and Rui needed to translate at times—translate in a somewhat irritated fashion—did not help the flow, or her grasp, either.

'Your signature is required here, and here,' said one of the lawyers, pointing to the first page of the document he had been explaining, and Sorcha realised her teach-in had come to an end.

The document, in which she guaranteed her responsibility for Club Marim's debts and contracts, was one of several which needed to be signed and initialled, page by interminable page. By the time she laid down the pen her hand felt as weary as her brain.

'*Tudo bem*?' Rui enquired when the elder of the two lawyers began an agitated search through the pile of papers.

'*Não*,' he mumbled, and reached for his briefcase. Much rummaging followed, until finally the man shrugged and spread his hands. 'We have neglected to bring a form which is necessary for the transfer,' he told Sorcha with an apologetic smile. 'It must be acquired from Lisboa, but——' he checked his watch '—the office there will now be closed. I shall ring tomorrow and request for the form to be posted. Will it be convenient if we deliver it for your signature on Saturday?'

'Sorry, I'm flying home on Friday afternoon,' she said. 'But if the form's put in the mail tomorrow, shouldn't it arrive the next morning?'

'Maybe. Maybe not.' She received another apologetic smile. 'This is Portugal, and here things do not always run to schedule.'

'Can't you postpone your departure until Saturday?' Rui enquired.

Sorcha shook her head. 'Sorry.'

'It's only one day.'

'One day too many.'

'You have a date with a boyfriend you're unwilling to pass up?' he demanded, his mouth hard with irritation.

'The date is with two boyfriends,' she replied.

Flinging her a furious look, he spoke to the lawyers in quick-fire Portuguese. 'If the form isn't signed it means everything must be put on hold,' he said, 'and we've been holding on for a couple of months already.'

'I regret I was unable to fly out here at the exact moment you clicked your fingers and that I must leave on Friday, as arranged,' Sorcha said, her words clipped and stony. 'But, although Club Marim may be more precious than jewels to you, I have other priorities.'

Rui muttered something that sounded like an oath. 'Suppose you had a flight mid-morning on Saturday?' he said doggedly. 'I could run you into the lawyers' office to sign the form first thing, and then take you on to the airport. You'd be in London mid-afternoon.'

'Which is too late.'

'Look, honey,' he growled, 'much as I hate to put a damper on your love-life, may I suggest——?'

'The form will probably arrive on Friday,' the younger of the lawyers broke in, his eyes jumping nervously between them as if he was wondering who would throw the first punch. He bundled the documents into a folder. 'We'll—how do you say in English?—keep the fingers crossed.'

'Let's do that,' Sorcha said succinctly.

Rui showed the visitors out. 'Jorge told me you could be exasperating,' he rasped, the minute the door had closed behind them, 'and——'

'If the form doesn't appear on time it can be sent to me in England,' Sorcha said sturdily, 'and I'll sign it and send it straight back.'

'By return of post?'

'Cross my heart and hope to die.'

Rui regarded her in silence for a moment or two, then he sighed. 'Thanks. Suppose we meet in the bar at eight and have a drink before dinner?' he said as she rose to leave.

Sorcha lifted surprised brows. 'You still want to wine and dine me?'

'I can't say the prospect makes me squirm with excitement,' he replied drily, 'but I need to eat and the food here is better than anything I can prepare.'

She grinned. 'All right—so long as you don't ask the barman to lace my drink with cyanide.'

'And risk the bad publicity which a murder on the premises would bring?' Rui protested. 'Not this baby.'

## CHAPTER THREE

THAT amicable working relationship was proving to be elusive, Sorcha brooded as she fastened her Aztec-patterned silk shirt and tucked it into the waistband of taupe suede trousers. She sighed. The last thing she needed in her life was another long-running battle, yet she had no intention of saying, 'Yes, sir. No, sir. Three bags full, sir,' simply to oblige Rui de Braganca. Why should she? He might possess the expertise and experience at Club Marim, but as co-director she was entitled to some kind of recognition, some kind of respect—and to some kind of an input.

Sorcha went into the bathroom to make up her face. It would not be a major input—all she wanted was the freedom to voice an occasional listened-to comment and maybe offer a suggestion which would be taken seriously—but a principle lay at stake. Bronze shadow was stroked on to her eyelids and her lashes were thickened with mascara. Had Rui never heard about respecting other people's opinions? Didn't he know about equality? When applied to the rest of mankind, she had no doubt that in both cases the answer would be an affirmative, yet, thanks to her stepfather's brainwashing, with her he was leery. Enormously. Adamantly. Frustratingly.

Her lips were coloured with a peach gloss. If anyone else had said they were unable to extend their stay it seemed certain he would have accepted it, but his immediate reaction had been that she was being flip and difficult. Sorcha grimaced at her reflection in the mirror. It had to be admitted that, in not telling him her reasons, maybe she *had* been difficult. As she fastened a fine gold chain around her neck and fitted golden hoops into her ears she decided she would explain, make amends and—with luck—win him over.

Furnished with green and white chintz-covered armchairs arranged around rattan tables and lush plants in ceramic tubs, the bar possessed a light, gardeny air. Like the restaurant, it overlooked the terrace which led down in broad stone steps to the swimming-pool. During the day the wall of glass stood open, but now it was closed. April evenings in the Algarve could be cool. However, the outdoors continued to feature, for in the darkness cleverly positioned spotlights picked out the softly swaying fronds of a palm, scarlet geraniums in serried tubs, the iridescent blue of the now tranquil water.

Although the bar was not full, several people were enjoying aperitifs, and when Sorcha walked in it took her a moment to find her escort. He was chatting to a couple of the guests, but when she approached he promptly excused himself and took her over to a table.

'What would you like to drink?' Rui asked as a broadly smiling waiter appeared.

'A white wine spritzer, please.'

'And I'll have a lager,' he said.

The waiter crossed to the bar, where he spoke to the bartender, who, with a quick look in their direction, started smiling broadly, too.

'They think I'm your girlfriend,' Sorcha said when the two men embarked on a discussion which obviously centred on their overlord and his companion.

'They do, and the reason they find it so rib-tickling is that I've never dined here with a woman before,' Rui replied sardonically.

'You're like Jorge; you don't mix business with pleasure?' she enquired.

He gave a curt laugh. 'You could say that.'

His face still bearing a wide smile, the waiter returned and served their drinks.

'I haven't had a chance before, but I'd like to thank you for phoning my mother,' Sorcha said when she had taken a sip. 'She told me how you've been calling each week or so to ask how she's getting along and if she's all right. That was kind. And she *is* all right. When my father walked out she had a nervous breakdown, and I wondered if she might go to pieces after Jorge died, but she hasn't.'

'It was a different situation and a different kind of relationship,' Rui remarked.

'True,' she agreed, and cast him a glance. His authoritative tone indicated that, when spilling the beans, her stepfather had also spoken about his marriage and her mother's earlier one, but in how much detail? she wondered.

Rui lifted his glass to his lips. 'Did you follow everything José said this morning?' he enquired.

His tone was casual, yet the glint in his eye warned the question could be yet another jab at her unsuitability as a Club Marim director. Sorcha's teeth ground together. She refused to confess to inadequacies to someone whose opinion of her already languished at ground level.

'Of course,' she replied airily.

'Liar,' he retorted. 'When José was listing the tax concessions you were totally lost.'

Sorcha took a hurried drink. What did she do, declare he was mistaken? But what if Rui then started to grill her on the subject?

'I may not have grasped every single point,' she said, 'but that doesn't mean——'

'You're a complete nincompoop?' he suggested, drawing out the syllables as he rolled the word around his mouth.

'It doesn't mean I won't understand the financial side once I have an opportunity to spend more time with José,' Sorcha said astringently.

Her reply silenced him for a moment or two, and he downed another mouthful of lager.

'When José asked whether, like me, you were happy to take your dividend money on a quarterly basis, you agreed,' Rui said, 'but if you'd prefer to receive a monthly cheque it can be arranged. And, if you'd like a sum on account to tide you over until the first payment arrives, that can be organised, too.'

'No, thanks.'

'There's no need to feel embarrassed. All of us have run short of funds in our time, and——'

'Must you be so patronising?' Sorcha demanded. 'Do I look as though I'm on the poverty line?'

Rui's eyes moved over her. 'No,' he admitted.

'And I'm not. You may be a whizz-kid at managing holiday developments, but,' she said, her voice rising in her impatience, 'I happen to be a whizz-kid artist.'

He glanced around. 'I'd be obliged if you didn't share what is supposed to be a private conversation with the entire clientele.'

Sorcha took a controlling breath. 'There are a couple of things you ought to know,' she said, her tone low and determined. 'Firstly, the reason

why I must go back on Friday is because I'm
taking the twins away for the weekend and we
leave straight after breakfast on Saturday. I'm
looking after them while my mother visits an old
friend in Dublin. If I don't return on time Mum'll
have to cancel her flight and the whole weekend
will need to be abandoned.'

'Why on earth didn't you say?' Rui protested.

'Because I don't like being pounced on.'

He frowned, and sampled his lager again.
'Where are you going with the twins?' he
enquired.

'To Devon. We're staying on a farm where you
can ride the horses, feed the pigs, see the cows
being milked, et cetera.'

'They should enjoy that,' he smiled.

'And so will I. I left home when they were
babies and we've never spent much time
together,' Sorcha said regretfully, 'so I'm looking
forward to getting to know them better. The
second thing I need to explain,' she continued,
'is that it was impossible for me to come out to
Portugal earlier because I've been tied up with
an exhibition of my paintings.'

Rui's brows came low. 'You had an exhibition?' he demanded.

'My second. It closed last Friday. At the time
of the funeral I was working flat out to get everything ready, and once the show was under way I
had to be at the gallery to meet clients. Personal

contact is good public relations and helps stimulate sales.'

'Did you sell much?' he queried.

'Almost ninety per cent,' Sorcha said, and beamed, unable to disguise her pleasure.

Rui gave a surprised laugh. 'You really are a whizz-kid painter,' he said wonderingly.

'I try.'

He pushed his hair from his brow. 'But according to Jorge you showed no sign of promise and had never sold a thing.'

'He didn't know I had.'

'You didn't tell him?'

'No, and I didn't tell my mother or Michael, either—though they know now. But on the day of the funeral they didn't, and as it wasn't the time or the place for explanations it meant I couldn't tell you about the exhibition, either.'

'But if Jorge'd realised you were successful——'

'He'd have been forced to revise his assessment of me,' Sorcha completed. 'I know. Yet, despite never having seen a single painting, he was always so *certain* I had no talent and continually slammed down my chances of making a living in what he maintained was a dumb-fool occupation anyhow. So when my career began to take off I thought "to hell with you" and remained silent.' She moved her shoulders. 'His attitude made me angry.'

'It also made you contrary,' Rui said, 'which is counter-productive.'

'Maybe,' she acknowledged, 'but I've grown up a lot since then. At the beginning my work didn't sell and for a while it seemed as though my stepfather could be right,' Sorcha recalled, then gave a sudden grin. 'You can't imagine how happy I was when people started to take an interest.'

'And Jorge was proved wrong?'

'That added spice,' she acknowledged.

Rui drank another mouthful from his glass. 'He said that when you were at art college your father supported you.'

She nodded. 'Dad had studied sculpture—until he realised he'd never be anything more than second-rate—so he was sympathetic. However, he runs a not very lucrative bookshop and couldn't spare much, so in the holidays I took whatever job I could find. Like the kissograms.' Sorcha waited for his smirk, but it did not come. 'And working on supermarket check-outs. And cleaning a gymnasium. And travelling the Greek islands, picking cucumbers and knocking olives out of trees.'

There was a crease in his left cheek which deepened when he grinned, and it deepened now. 'Greece sounds like fun,' Rui said. 'Which islands were you on?'

She was in the middle of telling him when the waiter came over to speak into his ear.

'Our table's ready,' Rui reported, so, after Sorcha had completed her itinerary and they had finished their drinks, they went through.

The garden theme of the bar had been continued into the restaurant, though with dark green velvet chairs and pink damask cloths the ambience was more luxurious. On each table a softly flickering candle illuminated cut-crystal glasses and gleaming, highly polished silver. They had just settled themselves when the head waiter appeared to provide parchment menus and make several recommendations; then the wine waiter came up. There was no sense of rushing, but with impeccable efficiency their orders were taken and the first course soon arrived.

'Are we being given VIP treatment?' Sorcha enquired, looking around to see whether the other tables were receiving equal attention.

'No, though the staff are aware that I'm appalled by sloppy service and that if anything's lacking I'll notice it and say so.' Rui gave a dry smile. 'I guess I'm a perfectionist where Club Marim's concerned, but if it's going to reach the top I have to be. When did your painting first get off the blocks?' he asked as they ate the prawn and avocado starter which both of them had chosen.

'A couple of years ago. A friend had a Sunday pitch on the railings outside Hyde Park and she suggested I should display a few pictures,' Sorcha explained. 'The owner of a Knightsbridge gallery happened to walk past and he offered to promote my work and, not much later, gave me a show. On that occasion over half of my paintings were cleared, plus I received a number of commissions. There were commissions from the last show, too. So now I've refunded my father, and am able to keep a roof over my head, plus feed and clothe myself—which is why I don't need an initial slug of money or more frequent payments.' She ate the last pinkly succulent prawn. 'Naturally any dividends I receive will be welcome, but they're not crucial.'

'At present a percentage of our profits is shunted into paying off the money borrowed to finance the redevelopment, but once that's been cleared the dividends will be significant,' Rui told her. 'Club Marim has excellent potential as a money-spinner, and the crux of it all is to keep standards high,' he stated, sounding like a teacher on a business-management course. 'If we cut corners there's no doubt that in the short-term profits would increase—but you don't go for quick bucks if you want a quality investment for the future.'

Sorcha sighed. She had had more than enough lectures for one day.

'If Club Marim isn't the last word in élitism, it's the end of civilisation as we know it?' she enquired sassily.

Rui frowned, but before he could reply the waiter arrived.

'*Cataplana* for madam,' he announced, setting a steaming casserole of clams, pork and fresh vegetables before her. 'And fillet steak, rare, for you, Senhor de Braganca.'

'Delicious,' Sorcha said, tasting her first mouthful of what the head waiter had recommended as a typical Portuguese dish.

She seemed to spend the entire meal exclaiming and praising, for the chocolate mousse which, in time, followed proved to be a delight, too. She also enjoyed the local cheeses which were served with dry biscuits and sweet white grapes.

'I'd like to come back and stay for longer,' Sorcha said as they were drinking coffee.

'When?' Rui enquired. 'And how long is longer?'

She thought for a moment. 'June, and I'll stay for a month.'

Carefully he replaced his cup on his saucer. 'A month?' he repeated.

Sorcha had been on the point of explaining how she would be coming in order to expand her portfolio, but the wariness in his voice made her change her mind.

'From the first to the thirtieth,' she enumerated.

Rui forced a smile. 'As you're doing so well with your painting, wouldn't it make more sense to concentrate on that?'

'And develop a one-track mind, like yours?' Sorcha protested. 'No, thanks.'

Although the thinning of his mouth showed her comment had hit home, he chose not to respond. 'I'm willing to continue running the show here,' he said determinedly, 'so all you need to do is——'

'All I need to do is ask the receptionist to reserve me a room tomorrow,' she cut in.

'The hotel's fully booked for June,' Rui said.

Sorcha's green eyes narrowed. Was he telling the truth? Possibly. But it was also possible he was being deliberately obstructive.

'Then I shall rent one of the villas—or are they all reserved, too?' she demanded.

'As a matter of fact, they are, but——' Rui raised a hand against her protests '—you can stay in the cottage. It belonged to a farm labourer, until a Dutch businessman with plans for renovation bought it,' he explained. 'The guy had constructed a pool, laid out gardens and got halfway with the internal improvements when his business suddenly folded. So Club Marim bought the property from him. It isn't as grand as the villas, but it's fully equipped. I've stayed there myself sometimes when I've been working late and been perfectly comfortable.' He hesitated. 'The only drawback is that it's at the top of the valley, set apart from the other properties and a bit remote.'

'Sounds ideal,' Sorcha declared, thinking how she preferred solitude for her painting.

Rui crumpled his table napkin in a large fist. 'A month can be a long time on your own; don't you think you could be bored?'

'Bored when I'll be finding out how everything ticks at the super-duper Club Marim?' she said archly. 'I doubt it.'

'How about your commissions—won't you still be working on them?'

'If so, I can always bring them along with me,' Sorcha replied, and sighed.

After her explanations the mood between them had seemed easier, yet she had not won him over. Far from it. Rui *still* regarded her as an unavoidable evil which had to be tolerated—barely. He continued to be wary of her disrupting things at Club Marim in some obscure, remote, heaven knew what way. As the waiter approached, the smallest curl at the edge of her lips gave her a wickedly mischievous smile. Sorcha sat straighter. If her fellow director expected disruptive, maybe she should oblige by giving him disruptive?

'More coffee, madam?' the waiter enquired.

'Please.' She reached across and placed her hand over Rui's hand. 'You know you were talking about us getting into bed together?' she said.

He frowned. 'I beg your pardon?'

'Bed,' she purred, with a seductive *femme fatale* pout. 'You must remember.'

Rui shot the waiter a wary look. 'Um...*sim*...I mean, yes, I do. But——'

'You want to marry me?' Sorcha enquired.

He snatched his hand away. 'That's a generous offer, but no.'

'More coffee, sir?' asked the waiter, who was blatantly listening.

'Black,' he muttered distractedly.

Sorcha heaved a dramatic and despairing sigh. 'So all you're interested in is my body? It's the old, old story, but if sex is what——'

'When I said what I did it was a figure of speech,' Rui interjected in a voice which sounded as though she had her hands fastened around his throat. 'And you know it!'

She opened huge innocent eyes. 'We're not going to make love?'

'No!'

'Madam?' The waiter was holding out a dish of after-dinner mints. She took one. 'Senhor de Braganca?'

'I can help myself,' Rui said tersely.

'Yes, *senhor*.' After setting down the dish, the waiter hovered. 'Is there anything else you require, *senhor*?'

'No!' he barked, and the man backed hurriedly away. Rui glared at her across the table. 'Thanks. Thanks a bunch,' he rasped. 'Thank you for providing the staff here with a vast amount of speculation and gossip.'

Sorcha grinned. 'I was only putting a kick into the proceedings. What's the matter?' she asked when he continued to glower. 'Are you worried one of your girlfriends might get to hear the gossip?'

'I don't have a girlfriend,' Rui grated. 'If you're nursing along something like Club Marim, there isn't time.'

'You not only work fourteen hours a day, you work every weekend, too?' she enquired.

'Not quite.'

'But you're so immersed in the place that you have as much social life as an amoeba?' Sorcha added cream to her cup. 'You take Club Marim far too seriously, and you're taking what I said too seriously, too. So there's a bit of talk, so what? It's no reason to go into orbit.'

Their second cups of coffee were drunk in silence, and a short while later they left the restaurant.

'There are some matters I need to attend to first thing tomorrow morning, so suppose we meet here at ten-thirty?' Rui suggested as they walked into the lobby.

Sorcha nodded. 'Thank you for being my escort,' she said politely when they reached the wide handsome staircase which led up to the bedrooms. Her eyes danced. 'I've enjoyed this evening. It was fun.'

'Glad you think so,' he muttered.

'*Guten abend*!' a voice suddenly cried, and they both looked up to see the talkative German woman from the minibus wiggling her fingers at the top of the stairs.

'Good evening,' Sorcha replied, then her mouth tweaked. The fun was not over yet. As the *hausfrau* started to make her way down towards them, she turned to Rui. 'I realise how desperate you are for me to be a sleeping partner,' she said in a bright, clear voice, 'but I'm afraid it's out of the——'

She got no further. His eyes glittering dangerously, he stepped forward, pushed his fingers into the thick silver-gold hair on either side of her head, drew her close and kissed her.

Held captive against the lithe length of his body, and with his mouth hard and commanding against hers, Sorcha felt her heart begin to pound. By provoking such a reaction she really *had* gone over the top, she thought frantically. She quivered. She had to get free. But when she raised her hands and pushed against his chest he refused to let her go. Sorcha knew she must try to escape again, yet a sudden and overwhelming inertia seemed to seep into her and take hold, and all she could do was stand there.

As if sensing the change in her, his kiss softened. The touch of his mouth on hers became warm and seductive, and when his tongue caressed her lips, coaxing them to open, Sorcha responded helplessly. Heat suffused her body and her senses began to swim. Any awareness of time and place dissolved. She forgot they were in a public place. She was blind to the German woman, watching wide-eyed as she walked past. All she knew was feel and touch and taste. The feel and touch and taste of Rui. With the sensual probing of his tongue, he seemed to know exactly how to arouse her. The blood beat in her head and a loose trembly feeling spread all over her. She was clutching desperately at the lapels of his jacket when, without warning, he drew back and the kiss was over as abruptly as it had begun.

Sorcha gazed at him. 'What—what do you think you're doing?' she stammered, feeling like a diver rocketing up for air.

'Shutting you up. What else?' Rui said harshly, and turned on his heel. 'Goodnight.'

## CHAPTER FOUR

As SORCHA closed her bedroom door and set off along the corridor she pinned on a smile. A jaunty one. In a couple of minutes' time she was due to meet her fellow-director and her manner would be—must be—casual. When he had left her last night she had been as breathless and bemused as a schoolgirl, but the kiss hadn't meant anything to him, nor to her. Sorcha's smile faltered. That she should have reacted so positively was unfortunate, and contrary to the norm. She might joke about sex, yet when it came to actual physical involvement her attitude was far more circumspect. So how did she explain her delirious co-operation in that impromptu, head-spinning clinch? Granted, Rui was an attractive and virile man and, like all healthy young women, she had her fair share of hormones, but even so... She frowned. Those hormones seemed to be working overtime, for she had gone to sleep thinking about the erotic pressure of his mouth on hers, and had thought about it immediately on waking. And now she seemed unable to shake off the memory.

Reaching the lobby, Sorcha refurbished her smile and looked around. Her escort was no-where in sight. As she waited she tugged at her white linen shorts and neatened the line of her sleeveless cerise top. She hoped Rui did not intend to hark back to the embrace and—horror of horrors—comment on how much she had appeared to enjoy it. If he showed the slightest in-clination that way she would need to rapidly change the subject and pray she did not blush. Searching in her shoulder-bag, Sorcha found her sunglasses and jammed them on. After acting the 'naughty nun' she had believed that nothing, but nothing, would ever faze her again, yet on several occasions recently she had found herself be-coming annoyingly rosy-faced.

'Senhorita Riordan,' a female voice said, and she turned to find Izabel walking towards her.

'Hello,' she smiled, but, again, received no smile in reply.

This morning the Portuguese girl was similarly dressed in knee-length shorts and a blouse, so it could not be her clothes which offended. Behind her dark glasses, Sorcha frowned. But had they ever been an issue? It seemed doubtful. Indeed, feminine intuition insisted that Izabel's coolness was inspired by something more personal. Though now she did not think it was her as a director of Club Marim that caused affront, but rather some aspect of her as a human being. Yet what aspect when they barely knew each other?

'Senhor de Braganca has had to visit Lagos unexpectedly and he said that if he was not back on time, I was to look after you,' the brunette enunciated in the impersonal tones of an airport announcer. 'He should soon return, but until then perhaps you would care to wait in my office? It is this way.'

With formal efficiency, Sorcha was seated in another pale-carpeted room and provided with a cup of coffee.

'Why has Rui gone to Lagos?' she asked, needing to break the taut silence which had begun to stretch out for what seemed like forever.

'He is visiting the suppliers of the roof tiles for the conference centre. The tiles are an unusual butterscotch colour of a high grade, and now the firm are saying that because they are a special order there could be a delay. So he has gone to insist the consignment is delivered, as promised.' His assistant gave a sudden grin. 'When Senhor de Braganca insists, it happens.'

Sorcha sipped her coffee. The brunette's affection for Rui had come over loud and clear, so could *he* be the reason why she was so aloof? As she was a new woman in his life, did Izabel regard her as competition? If only she knew! she thought wryly. But had the waiter already circulated what he had overheard? Could one of the staff have seen them kissing, and did that mean any gossip was of a red-hot love-affair? Sorcha nibbled at her lip. Her mischief-making in the restaurant had never been intended to cause anyone real distress, so maybe she should issue a disclaimer?

'Rui seems very committed to Club Marim,' she remarked as she wondered how an explanation could best be phrased.

'He has a management style I believe in English is called ''hands-on'', which means he works fourteen hours a day,' Izabel said proudly, then gave a brittle smile. 'But do you imagine he would not be committed, when he has provided all the ideas, the drive, the impetus here? Maybe you are not supposed to speak ill of the dead, but I feel that in fairness to Senhor de Braganca I must put the record straight and tell you that your stepfather—— '

'Strode around like he was the big boss but, in fact, did nothing,' Sorcha broke in.

'You—you know?' the brunette faltered.

'Yes, though I've always been aware that where hard work and dedication were concerned he was a wash-out.'

'A wash-out?'

'My stepfather was no good. A failure,' she defined pungently.

Izabel looked confused. She had been expecting her revelation to produce a string of dismayed protests, not blunt agreement.

'I understood you and Senhor Almeida were—were devoted to each other,' she said hesitantly.

Sorcha gave a short laugh. 'You understood wrong!'

'But he told me——'

'He told you lies.' Her face clouded. 'He told you how he might have liked it to be, but it wasn't. I didn't like him.'

'Neither did I,' Izabel said.

At the confession a barrier between them seemed to lift. All coldness vanished, and now the Portuguese girl visibly warmed and demonstrated a wish to be friends.

'Rui will be showing you the villas this morning,' she said. 'I would love to live in such style——' she sighed '—and perhaps if Arnaldo and I save hard one day it will happen.'

'Arnaldo?' Sorcha queried.

'He is my boyfriend and we are to become engaged on my birthday in two months' time,' she explained, knocking the 'Izabel loves Rui' scenario for six.

Now the brunette's chatter moved to her soon-to-be fiancé. As they drank their coffee she described Arnaldo, whom, it appeared, possessed the looks of a matinée idol and the personality of a patron saint, then moved happily on to talking about their wedding, which was to take place the following spring. She was in the midst of describing the dress she planned when the door opened and Rui strode in.

He greeted them both, then turned to Sorcha. 'My apologies,' he said, 'but I was forced to go and read the Riot Act over some tiles.'

'You were successful?' she enquired.

'Yes,' he replied, and she and Izabel exchanged a smile. He looked at the steel watch which was strapped to his broad wrist. 'Shall we be off?'

Sorcha rose and, after saying goodbye to the Portuguese girl, she went with him to where the jeep was parked in its designated place.

'How did you get on with Izabel?' Rui asked as she climbed into the passenger-seat. 'Was she . . . agreeable?'

'Very.' Sorcha grinned. 'It wasn't my clothes she disliked, or me. It was Jorge.'

He switched on the ignition. 'Jorge?' he repeated in a somewhat careful voice.

'Yes. Izabel's the first female I've met who didn't automatically fall under his spell. And, once she realised I hadn't been an admirer of his, either, everything between us went swimmingly.'

'Did she say why she disliked him?' he enquired, reversing on to the road.

Sorcha shrugged. 'I assume she saw through his charm.'

For a moment Rui seemed about to speak and maybe to argue, but then he changed his mind.

Had he been going to defend her stepfather? she wondered. Had he been on the brink of pointing out that, whatever her and Izabel's distaste, he had enjoyed a close relationship with his employer?

'First we'll visit the tennis complex, and then I'll take you around the indoor sports centre,' was what Rui did say.

Sorcha assumed their 'visiting' the tennis complex would mean a stop and maybe a call in at the reception office and an inspection of the courts. It was not so. Rui simply drove past. And 'taking her around' the sports building was a matter of their circumnavigating the outside of that, too. Next, they motored to the embryo conference centre, where all she managed was a from-the-jeep glimpse at the construction site, before Rui sped on to the northern part of the development. Here, with a waft of his hand, he indicated the tract of rough land which had yet to be developed.

'Now I'll show you the villas,' he said.

'You've chased up the tiles, but is there some other crisis which is crying out for your helping hand?' Sorcha enquired as they headed into the leafy lanes of the residential area.

Rui frowned. 'No.'

'Then would it inconvenience you greatly if my tour was not quite so whistle-stop? Would you mind if I actually got to see inside a villa?'

His lips compressed. 'Sure,' he agreed, 'though it'll mean us going back to the hotel in order to get the keys to one which is unoccupied.'

'Then let's do it.' Sorcha shone an on-off smile. 'After all, it's not as though we're talking in terms of a thousand-mile detour.'

The keys were collected and they drove to a house on a wooded corner site, which had a garden filled with rose-pink hibiscus and spectacular views of the sea. Unlocking the heavy oak front door, Rui led her through the four luxurious bedrooms, each with *en-suite* bathroom, the ice-white kitchen with its dazzling array of up-to-the-minute appliances, the split-level, cream-carpeted living area.

'Izabel told me the villas were stylish, and they are,' Sorcha enthused as he showed her the patio and built-in barbecue area. 'I'm very impressed. I've been impressed with everything.'

'Good,' Rui said, with what was his first smile of the morning.

'However, with me around, Club Marim now has the chance to become even *more* impressive,' she added pertinently.

He jiggled the car keys in his hand. 'That's the cottage,' he said, pointing across the valley to where the white walls of a low building could be seen among trees on the distant hillside. 'Would you care to look around it?'

'No, thanks,' Sorcha replied, for his offer was enough. 'I'd prefer to keep it as a surprise.'

'Then suppose we go to the beach?' Rui suggested.

Back down the hill they sped, and past the hotel. The narrow road to the bay ended in a circular turning place above and to one end of the arc of sand, and here they stopped.

Rui indicated the dramatic yellow cliffs, the secluded beach, the turquoise waters of the Atlantic Ocean.

'Does it meet with your approval?' he enquired.

Sorcha grinned. 'Oh, yes.'

'And with mine,' he said, and smiled again.

'How about a paddle?' she suggested.

He looked at her in astonishment. 'A paddle?'

'You take off your shoes and socks, and——'

'I know what paddling means,' Rui interrupted.

'Well, then? I have some questions about Club Marim,' Sorcha went on, 'and it'd be just as easy for me to ask them outdoors in the sunshine as in your office.'

He considered the proposition. It was years since he had paddled, but maybe he had rushed her tour and maybe he should be more amenable, he thought. And maybe his life was too much work and no play.

'Why not?' he said.

Apart from a couple with a toddler who were building sand-castles at the far end, the beach was deserted. Walking down to the water's edge, they shed their shoes and Rui rolled up the bottoms of his jeans.

'It's freezing!' Sorcha yelped as she made a tentative foray into the shallows.

'The water may be a little cool,' he said, coming in behind her, 'but once you get used to it——'

'If you stayed in long enough to get used to it your feet would drop off,' she vowed.

'You're too soft,' Rui declared and, with a grin, he bent, scooped up a handful of water, and splashed it on to her bare legs.

'Hey!' Sorcha protested.

'I'm getting you acclimatised.'

'Don't bother!'

'It's no trouble,' he assured her, bending again and laughing as she backed away.

He went after her, and Sorcha's retreat quickened. A chase began. Through the ankle-deep water she cantered, going parallel with the shoreline and keeping a safe distance from Rui, until, all of a sudden, she cantered into a hole.

'Oh!' she exclaimed, coming to a full stop.

Although the water was deeper, it did not reach her shorts. Sorcha would have remained perfectly dry if, at the same moment that she stopped, Rui had not trawled up a second handful from the sea and tossed it at her. But this time, instead of wetting her legs, he spattered her from her shoulder and down one side.

'Thanks!' she said indignantly.

He gave a startled laugh. 'Hell,' he said, 'I never meant to do that.'

Her eyes suspicious, Sorcha studied him. That he should have drenched her did seem to have been just bad timing, but if he had done it on purpose she would retaliate—by drenching him, all over.

'Honest?' she enquired.

'Honest,' Rui replied, 'and I apologise.'

Recognising his sincerity, Sorcha smiled. 'Humbly?' she asked, her eyes dancing.

'And meekly. And abjectly. If we were on dry land I would grovel at your feet,' he proclaimed.

'You're overdoing it,' she warned.

Rui grinned, the crease in his cheek deepening. 'OK, but I am sorry.'

'It's no big deal,' she said, and looked down at the damp patches on her top and shorts. 'If I stay in the sun I'll soon dry.'

Sorcha Riordan might be a bit of a handful, Rui reflected as they walked back up on to the sand, but he admired the easy way she had accepted being soaked. Mistake or not, there were plenty of women who would have complained bitterly and accused him of ruining their appearance and their clothes. A handful; the word

repeated itself in his head and his gaze went to
her silk top. The wet material had moulded itself
to one perfectly round breast which, because the
water he had thrown had been cold, was centred
by a thrusting pointed nub. His palms began to
itch. He wanted to close his hand around that
high, firm curve. He wanted to brush his thumb
across the tempting promise of that nipple. He
wanted to bare her breast, and cover it with his
mouth and suck fiercely at the tender skin.

Pushing his hands into his trouser pockets, Rui
turned to frown out at the ocean. What was he
thinking about? This disturbing flight of fancy
could only be because he had kissed her the pre-
vious evening, he thought grimly. Though *why*
he had kissed her he did not know. When Sorcha
had started to tease him he could have simply
walked away. He expelled a heavy sigh. It was
obvious that he was missing a woman in his life
and in his bed, but he had neither the time nor
the inclination for a relationship. Not yet. Not
for another two years, at least.

'Are bedrooms being built at the conference
centre?' Sorcha asked, beside him.

'Er—yes,' he said, startled. 'There's to be a
wing of twenty. Didn't I say?'

'When you were driving me past at the speed
of light? No. It must have slipped your mind.'

Rui frowned. 'There'll be twenty double-
bedded rooms, but, as the idea is that the con-

ferences will, in the main, take place out of the peak holiday season, participants will also be accommodated in the hotel.'

'What is the peak season on the Algarve?' Sorcha enquired.

Grateful to be able to channel his thoughts back to business—and grateful that her blouse was beginning to dry—Rui explained. She had further questions: about the number of staff, about the ownership of the villas, whether Club Marim provided any kind of entertainment for its visitors. He was forced to admit that they were sensible, apposite questions, and—as they drove back to the hotel, and all through the lunch which they subsequently ate in the coffee shop beside the pool—he answered them.

Early afternoon they went to his office, where Rui spread a sheaf of blueprints out on his desk.

'You remember I showed you the rough land?' he said.

'I remember the blur from the jeep,' Sorcha replied.

'Yes. Well, a large part of it is scheduled to become a golf course. This golf course.'

'Classy,' she remarked, joining him to look down at a drawing of the entire course, which incorporated a stream, lily-strewn ponds, and numerous stands of pine trees.

'Antonio's been liaising with the course designers, who reckon it'll take around eighteen months to construct, together with clubhouse and car parking, so we're thinking in terms of starting towards the middle of next year,' Rui told her. 'By then the conference centre'll be functioning, so I'll be able to take an interest.'

Sorcha cast him a look. 'You mean you'll be able to work not just fourteen hours a day, but the entire twenty-four?' she enquired.

'I figured on twenty-five,' he replied, with the glimmer of a smile. He drew up a chair. 'Sit down,' he said, 'and take a look.'

With his eyes shining and his hands sweeping back and forth, Rui started to explain the drawings. They were sitting so close together that, when he gestured, his bare arm occasionally brushed against hers and sometimes his thigh grazed her thigh. Sorcha edged her chair away. His touch might be casual—and he was so wound up in his plans that he did not notice—yet it still disturbed.

'Damn,' Rui muttered when the telephone rang and interrupted them, though throughout the afternoon it was destined to ring incessantly.

After familiarising her with the golf course he produced plans for the remainder of the land. Designs had been drawn up for a number of ultra-select, mouth-wateringly luxurious villas to be built around a small lake.

'It looks as though they'll blend well into the surroundings,' Sorcha remarked, for the villas were to be sited among tall trees and the plot skilfully landscaped.

'That was an essential. The Algarve is a glorious stretch of coast, yet some developers care nothing for the environment and have thrown up eyesores which, frankly, need a large bomb detonated under them,' Rui said, flinging his arms around in disgust. 'However, like everything else at Club Marim, the villas are tasteful and harmonise with the scenery.'

'And, as with everything else, I have the last word on the villas—and the veto,' she said quietly.

While Sorcha admired his enthusiasm—and his plans—yet again he had been telling her what *he* intended would happen. He had not asked her whether she approved, nor requested a comment. This could have been due to his being so engrossed, but, nevertheless, a reminder of her existence seemed appropriate.

His head whipped round in sudden alarm and he stared at her. 'You want to veto them?' Rui demanded.

'No, but——'

'I should think not,' he grated, with a look which said that if she had she could have run the risk of severe personal injury. Rising from his chair, he strode round to the other side of the desk, where he stopped and faced her. 'Why were you such a brat when you were young?' he enquired.

'As—as you've already realised, it was a rebellion against my stepfather,' Sorcha faltered, thrown off balance by a question which had seemed to have come out of the blue.

'But what the hell was going on inside your head?'

'I was an adolescent and——'

'And adolescence can be a difficult time,' Rui cut in impatiently. 'But whereas most kids in your kind of situation would have settled for throwing the occasional rock, you ran around with a meat cleaver for years and years.'

Alarm bells rang. No matter how much those at the receiving end might have complained about her bad behaviour, no one had ever given it more than a superficial analysis, nor thought to query the protracted amount.

'I'm half-Irish, and the Celts are known for their fighting spirit,' Sorcha said, dashing off a smile.

'That's an excuse, not a reason.'

'And I suppose I've always had a wilful streak,' she said, in a tone which was meant to signal that the conversation was over.

Rui did not comply. Instead he studied her as though she were something happening in a test-tube, then shook his head. 'I don't buy it.'

'It was a long time ago and it's water under the bridge.' Sorcha flashed another smile, this one trimmed with steel. 'So, Sherlock Holmes, I'd be grateful if you'd turn off your questing mind.'

'But——'

'End of discussion,' she snapped. 'OK?'

Rui rubbed a finger back and forth across his lower lip, drawing her attention to the contrast of its full, almost voluptuous curve with the thinner severity of his upper one. Those were the lips which had kissed her, Sorcha found herself thinking. The lips which had played such havoc with her nerves.

'It's ironical,' he said. 'Although Jorge was desperate to exert control over you, when he was alive you made sure he never managed it. But, now that he's dead, the guy's in there and manipulating.'

Her spine stiffened. 'How?' she demanded.

'Your connection with Club Marim means that every time you come out to Portugal he made it happen. And, however you spend your dividend money, you spent it courtesy of him.' Rui gave a wry laugh. 'Jorge is probably sitting on a cloud somewhere, congratulating himself for having won out in the end. Suppose we meet up for a drink before dinner again, same time, same place?' he went on.

Sorcha sat stock-still. All she could see was an image of her stepfather rubbing his hands together for glee and smugly chuckling. He continued to pull strings? Her life was still being affected by him? Her head throbbed. She had not viewed her inheritance from this angle before, but now her green eyes darkened. Jorge would not be allowed to retain any influence, she thought mutinously. None whatsoever.

'Dinner?' she repeated, suddenly becoming aware that Rui was watching her.

'In the restaurant.'

Sorcha pushed back her chair. 'No, thanks. I—I thought I'd order something from room service and have an early night.'

'Are you feeling all right?' he enquired as she headed for the door.

She paused and dredged up a smile. 'I'm fine. It's just that—well, the pace here has been hectic, and if I'm to be at my best with the twins I need to recharge my batteries. I'll see you tomorrow before I leave. Bye.'

Her suitcase was packed and waiting to be collected. Her flight ticket and passport were accessible in her bag. Sorcha inspected her watch. In half an hour the minibus would ferry her back to the airport. Locking her room, she went down the staircase and across the lobby. There was just enough time to say goodbye to Rui and—she frowned—to break the news.

'At last,' he said as she walked into his office. 'The form arrived from Lisbon this morning, but although I called your room several times there was no answer. And you weren't having breakfast in the coffee shop or taking a dip in the pool, either.'

'I've been down to Praia do Marim,' she said as he extracted the document from a pile of correspondence. Sorcha signed her name in the requisite places, then gave an apologetic smile. 'I'm afraid that all this transfer business will need to be gone through again. You see, I've decided to sell my shareholding in Club Marim. This morning I——'

His hands gripping the edge of his desk, Rui leant forward. 'You've decided to sell?' She had expected some spontaneous sign of delight—an unstoppable smile, if not a triumphant guffaw— but his expression was impassive and gave nothing away. 'Why?' he demanded.

Sorcha hooked a strand of fair hair behind her ear. 'As you pointed out, I don't know the first thing about the holiday industry,' she began carefully, 'and——'

'You mustn't let that influence you. You mustn't be swayed by anything I've said,' Rui interrupted, and readjusted the blotter pad on his desk. 'Because Jorge never showed the slightest inclination to take part in the decision-making or help with the running of Club Marim, I assumed it'd be the same with you,' he started to explain. 'I thought you'd be content for me to be in sole charge and that you'd rubber-stamp everything I said.' He scowled. 'Also, I guess, I'd fallen into the trap of thinking my views were the only views, so, when you arrived here and indicated the desire to put forward your opinions, it took me by surprise and I resented it. And you resented me——' he searched for an apt English phrase '—not giving you your place?'

'I resented the way you lorded it over me,' Sorcha said, in a more explicit condemnation.

Rui realigned the blotter pad again. 'I was wrong.'

'I still want to opt out,' she said, her voice softer because she recognised he was a proud man and that neither his admissions nor the apology had come easily.

'Sorcha, the dividends will provide security for you and, in time, for your children, too,' he said gravely. 'You won't become a millionairess overnight, but you will have a good income and reasonably soon. Also Club Marim has yet to be fully developed, and whatever you receive for your shares now will be peanuts compared to what you'd get if you hung on for, say, five years.'

'So selling will be another of life's missed opportunities,' Sorcha said glibly.

Rui thrust her a sharp look. 'Yesterday you were keen to become involved here, so why the sudden change of heart?'

'It's a woman's prerogative,' she recited, then, hearing herself sound too frivolous, added, 'Until now I haven't had much time to think about exactly what my inheritance entails.'

'And you have thought—seriously?' he demanded.

'Yes, and I want out. The bank manager said he's sure that the client who was originally interested in buying Club Marim will be interested again, so——'

'You went to see the bank manager?' Rui interrupted.

Sorcha nodded. 'In Praia do Marim. You remember you told me how he had a client who——'

'Did he give you his client's name?' he asked curiously.

'No. All he said was that the man represents a company which owns other holiday developments on the Algarve.'

'So the client could be a large foreign conglomerate or some cowboy builder which, in either case, would have meant Club Marim going down-market,' Rui muttered.

'Why?' Sorcha asked.

'Because, for them, the number-one concern is maximising profits.'

'You don't know that,' she protested, then paused. 'What do you mean "would have meant"?'

A smile bloomed in the corner of his mouth. In instructing her to ignore his remarks and then making sure she understood the financial disadvantage in so rapidly disposing of her shares, he had acted fairly and honourably. But now he was free to state his interest.

'Because I shall buy your holding,' Rui told her. 'Independent assessors will need to be brought in to decide the market value, but I'll pay whatever sum they quote.'

Sorcha looked at him in bewilderment. 'You can afford it?' she asked.

'Yes. It'll mean liquidating all my assets, but I'm happy to do that.' His smile spread. 'Overjoyed.'

'But the holding must be worth a lot of money, and as manager here you—you can't have been earning such a high salary,' she faltered.

'My background is wealthy and I have private funds,' Rui said impatiently. 'Funds which, over the years, I've invested and increased. Increased sufficiently to be able to buy you out.'

Sorcha frowned. 'As I lack any business training,' she said, 'perhaps you could tell me whether, if you're selling something, it's common practice to settle for the first offer?'

'No.' Rui's jaw hardened. 'But it'd be sacrilege to let the club fall into the hands of some foreign conglomerate or a cowboy builder.'

'Your idea that the anonymous client must fit into one of those categories is pure conjecture,' she replied.

'Maybe, but you can't——'

'Can't what? Can't try and get the best possible price for my shares?' Sorcha protested.

He sank his head into his hands. 'The first time I saw you I knew you'd screw things up for me in one way or another. I knew it,' he muttered.

'You looked at me and your immediate thought was that I was a wrecker?' she enquired indignantly.

His eyes met hers. 'If you really want to know, my immediate thought was, what a stunning girl——' Rui stopped in a grim pause '—I wonder what her breasts are like.'

Hot colour invaded her cheeks. 'I have no wish to screw anything up for you,' Sorcha told him tightly. 'By selling to the highest bidder, all I'm doing is selling in the usual manner.'

'All you're doing is not giving a damn about Club Marim,' he retorted, 'and raking in as much cash as you can. What are you going to do with it? Treat yourself to a fancy apartment? Splash out on a sports car? Fritter it away on designer clothes and Caribbean holidays?'

She avoided his gaze. 'That's my business.'

'And Club Marim is mine. This place is as vital to me as the air I breathe,' Rui declared, sounding very Latin, very intense, very emotional. Pushing himself out of his chair, he began to prowl restlessly around the room. 'Club Marim is a part of *me*.'

'You're being melodramatic,' Sorcha declared. 'Besides, if you come up with the best offer——'

'And if I don't?' he demanded.

Her lips jammed together. Her only desire was to get rid of her shares. Period. She did not want to be made to feel as if she was committing some kind of a crime. She refused to succumb to his emotional blackmail.

'Club Marim can still be part of you,' she said impatiently. 'After all, you'll continue to own forty-nine per cent, and whoever buys my holdings could well be delighted for you to continue as manager.'

'And even if that happens, you reckon my ideas would stand a chance? You think the club will be allowed to advance as planned?' Rui gave a terse laugh. 'Not on your life! As the major shareholder, whoever takes over will push through their decisions, for good or for ill,' he added darkly.

'Sounds as though, in retrospect, having me as fellow-director wasn't such a catastrophe, after all,' Sorcha remarked.

'In retrospect, you were the lesser of two evils,' he retorted. 'Just.'

They were glaring at each other like scorpions in a bottle, when the telephone rang.

'Manuel's arrived,' Rui reported after exchanging a few sentences of Portuguese. 'Apparently there are roadworks on the way to the airport, so he's eager to leave early. I'll tell him you'll be out in a minute. What about June?' he demanded when he had jettisoned the phone. 'Do you still intend to visit?'

Sorcha frowned. 'Do you think the sale of my shares will be finalised by then?' she enquired.

'I doubt it. Putting a figure on their value will take time. Likewise any haggling which may then follow,' he added harshly.

'Then I'd like to come and stay at the cottage, and do some painting.' She hesitated. 'If that's OK with you.'

Rui gave a curt laugh. 'Honey, I'm not the one who has the veto around here—remember?'

# CHAPTER FIVE

THE glitter of the morning sun on the water was beginning to dazzle. The temperature had risen, too. Peeling off the shirt which covered her leopard-print halterneck, Sorcha tugged the brim of her straw hat lower over her eyes, and repositioned herself on the steps where she was sitting. Again, she concentrated on the fishing boat tied up on the far side of the harbour. For fifteen minutes she sketched, then her pencils were abandoned and she delved into her bag. Because she had wanted to avoid people goggling and breathing down her neck, she had risen early and come straight here—but now she was hungry.

Locating an apple, Sorcha polished it on her shorts. How much longer would it be before the final bid had been made for her stake in Club Marim? she wondered as she took a bite. She wished it would happen *soon*. Like today. And then the actual sale could proceed and, at last, she would be free.

Shortly after her return to England two months ago Rui had telephoned to say he had contacted a firm of valuers who had agreed to study the accounts, calculate future earnings, and pronounce on how much her holding was worth. They were to start the next day but, he had told her again, their investigations would take time. Sorcha munched at the apple. The time taken had turned out to be lengthy. Weeks had passed without any figure being produced. When Rui had rung with his regular updates he had insisted this was reasonable, but for her each day she waited represented a frustrating delay. Eventually three weeks ago, which was a fortnight before her arrival in Portugal, the valuers had given a sum.

'Is it acceptable?' her fellow-director had wanted to know, and Sorcha's answer had been a prompt affirmative. 'It's acceptable to me, too,' he had said, 'but I'll ask the bank manager to notify his client.'

After considering the matter the client had topped the figure by a small percentage. In turn, Rui had made a higher offer, and now the ball was back in the client's court where, for the last ten days, it had stayed.

'Whoever it is will need to do their sums again, consult with accountants, weigh the pros and cons,' Rui had said irritably when Sorcha had complained about their dilly-dallying. 'You may reach your decisions in the space between dusk and dawn, but not everyone is so inclined.'

She tossed the apple core to a waiting seagull. Because Rui's manner had been abrasive and formal, when he had invited her to dine with him

she had declined. He had only asked out of a
sense of duty, and she refused to waste her time—
and his—making stilted conversation. And, as
they had gone their separate ways in the evenings, so they had had sparse contact during the
day. After her early morning sketching Sorcha
had fallen into the routine of boarding a bus and
visiting towns and villages up and down the coast.
It had been dusk before she had returned to Club
Marim. Her aim, so she told herself, was to find
artistic inspiration, and had nothing to do with
avoiding Rui—whose attitude made her feel like
the irksome and wayward child she had once
been.

'Finished work already?' a cheery English voice
enquired, and Sorcha looked up to find a fair-
haired young man in a 'RIGHT TO PARTY' T-shirt
grinning down at her.

She had seen him before. Sometimes he had
been buying fish from the boats, or chatting to
local youths in the square.

'I'm allowed breakfast,' she protested.

'Then have a proper one. Bacon, scrambled
eggs and tomato, accompanied by fresh
wheatmeal toast and hot coffee. How does that
sound?'

'You're making my mouth water,' Sorcha confessed with a smile.

'Come to Ruffians,' the young man said,
naming a bar-cum-café on Praia do Marim's

cobbled main street. With tables set beneath the shade of a spreading tree, it was a popular place with the tourists. 'I'm Mark Halston, the proprietor,' he added when she hesitated.

'You own it?' she enquired, surprised because he could only be in his early twenties and seemed far too nonchalant.

'My father owns it and I run it,' he amended. Whisking an imaginary hat from his head, he bent low. 'Your table awaits, ma'am.'

Sorcha packed away her drawing materials and went with him across the square. Although she did not usually eat much in the mornings, today she felt hungry—and, if he was drumming up business, she was happy to oblige. Also Mark Halston seemed to be a pleasant individual and, after Rui's formality, his carefree air was appealing. When they reached the café he pulled a chair out from a table and, as she sat down, bowed low again. Taking a seat opposite, he clicked his fingers and a white-aproned waiter, who had been on the point of handing the menu to another couple, swerved and came over to them.

'You're joining me?' Sorcha said, startled when her escort ordered breakfast for two. 'You don't have work to do?' she protested, for most of the other tables were occupied and the waiter was operating alone.

'Nah, Laszlo can manage. Besides, I'd rather sit here in the sunshine with you and chat.'

As they ate the food, which appeared after a somewhat lengthy wait, Mark Halston chatted about anything and everything, made non-stop jokes, and paid her increasingly flowery compliments. He was an actor. A ham actor, Sorcha thought, wryly listening to what could only be described as a performance.

'I've enjoyed my breakfast,' she said as she drained her coffee-cup. 'Thanks for suggesting it.'

'And it was on the house,' he grinned.

Sorcha shook her head. 'I want to pay, and if you don't let me I shan't eat at Ruffians again,' she went on when he began to argue.

'Then pay, pay—and you'll come for dinner this evening?' he implored, all on a breath.

For a moment she hesitated, then she nodded. 'So long as it's understood that I pay for myself, then.'

Mark rolled theatrically pained eyes to the sky. 'It is.'

By ten o'clock that evening Sorcha had discovered that, pleasant though he was, a little of Mark Halston went a long way. Again he had joined her, leaving the rushed Laszlo to cope alone, and again his conversation had been peppered with jokes and overdone flattery. Why had she ever agreed to dine at Ruffians? she wondered wearily. Because she had been fed up with eating alone at the cottage every evening. But now solitary dining seemed infinitely preferable to dining with a young man who talked non-stop and who also, thanks to his lavish consumption of wine, was becoming increasingly amorous. As he lifted her hand and noisily pressed a kiss to each of her fingers in turn, Sorcha squirmed. They were seated in the open, with people at nearby tables and strolling past, and it was embarrassing to be courted in such a flamboyant and tacky manner.

'I'd like my bill,' she told him, hastily retrieving her hand. 'Then I must go.'

Mark gestured along the street to where a purple neon sign flashed on and off. 'But I thought we'd move on to the disco and boogie the night away?'

Sorcha shook her head. 'I want to make an early start in the morning and that means a relatively early night. May I pay my bill, please?' she said, forestalling Laszlo.

'How about half an hour at the disco?' Mark started to appeal when her account had been settled, then he stopped to give a sudden smile. 'Hi, Dad,' he said.

A Mercedes car had pulled up outside the café and a burly, grey-haired man in a navy blazer and flannels was climbing out.

'Hello there,' the new arrival replied.

'Join us for a drink,' Mark insisted, and with eager haste he instructed Laszlo to bring another glass and another bottle of wine. 'Sorcha, meet my father,' he said. 'Dad, this is Sorcha Riordan.'

'Terence Halston,' the older man said, greeting her jovially, and sat down beside her.

A few minutes of small talk about Praia do Marim followed, but when the waiter appeared with the wine Sorcha placed her hand over her glass.

'Not for me, thanks,' she said. 'I'm going.'

'Right now?' Mr Halston protested.

''Fraid so. It was nice to meet you,' she said, and nodded at his son. 'Bye.'

'Mark'll drive you back in the Merc,' Mr Halston offered as she got to her feet.

'No, thanks,' Sorcha said hastily. Not only did the amount the young man had drunk put him well over the safety limit, but there seemed little doubt that if they were alone together his amorous advances would become even more advanced. 'I like to walk,' she said, and, with a quick smile, she hurried away.

Sorcha crossed the square and headed up the hill. A hundred yards on and the lights and bustle of the village lay behind her. To one side, the squat houses were shuttered and silent. To the other, beyond a wall, the cliff fell down to the inky blackness of the sea. She was listening to the pad of her solitary footsteps and the gentle plash of the waves on the rocks far below, when another noise intruded. A vehicle was coming up the narrow road. Sorcha moved into the side and kept on walking. She expected the vehicle to drive past, but as it drew level it slowed. Had Mark decided to make chase? she wondered. She cast a quick irritated glance sideways, but saw it was a jeep. Jeeps were the ubiquitous form of transport on the Algarve, and to her most of them looked the same. Yet hadn't this one been parked on the square, and hadn't the engine been gunned as she had gone by? Alarm stirred within her. Praia do Marim had seemed so safe, but all of a sudden Sorcha was aware of being a woman alone in the night.

'Get in,' a male voice called over the noise of the engine.

Accept a lift from a stranger? Take a ride with someone who could have seen her, earmarked her, followed her? Did he think she had been born yesterday? Fixing her eyes determinedly ahead, Sorcha lengthened her stride. But she had only gone a few yards when a surge from behind her indicated that the jeep had accelerated, too.

'Get in,' the driver commanded again as the vehicle came up alongside.

He sounded impatient, as though if she did not obey he might *make* her obey. Sorcha's heart began to hammer. Only last week she had read

a newspaper report about a girl who had been
abducted and found later, naked and strangled
in a ditch. She walked faster—and the jeep accelerated again. If she screamed, would anyone
in the shuttered houses hear her? she wondered,
her alarm billowing. And if they heard, would
they come to the rescue in time?

Behind her, the jeep braked and the engine was
switched off. A moment later the door opened
and there was the clatter of feet on cobbles as
the driver jumped out. Sorcha's stomach hol-
lowed. What did she do now? The village—so
near, and yet so far away—offered safety, but
how could she run back when he was in her path?
She must run forward. She had gulped in a
breath, tensed, and was about to make a dash
for it when a large hand suddenly landed on her
shoulder. She froze. She was trapped. He had
her at his mercy.

'What the hell are you playing at?' her captor
demanded.

Recognising the voice, Sorcha spun around.
'Rui!' she bleated, weak with relief. 'Thank
goodness! I thought you were someone who was
going to kidnap me. I know it sounds silly——'
she flashed a smile '—it does to me now,
but——'

'I meant, what are you playing at with the
Halstons?' he cut in.

'The Halstons?' she enquired.

'You had breakfast with Mark this morning and dinner this evening and, for all I know, could have been doing so for the past week,' he said, his voice rough with irritation. 'And you've just been fraternising with his father.'

Sorcha stood taller. She did not consider the exchange of a few sentences to be fraternising, but she did object to being attacked like this.

'What if I have?' she retorted, then her brow creased. 'How did you know?'

Striding back to the jeep, Rui gestured for her to climb inside. He waited until she was seated and then, with an angry flick of his wrist, twisted the ignition key. With a squeal of tyres, they shot away.

'José spotted you when he happened to be in Praia do Marim this morning, and when I was driving home tonight I saw Mark seducing you by——' his brown eyes were contemptuous '—kissing your fingers.'

Sorcha flushed. 'You may have been driving home, but it's clear you stopped to spy,' she said tartly, furious to discover he had witnessed the skin-crawling incident. 'How long were you sitting there—one hour or two? Maybe you used binoculars and took long-range photographs?'

'I just——' Rui began, but she allowed him no access.

'If I dine with Mark Halston, or with anyone else, for that matter, it's my choice,' she declared.

His hands tightened around the steering-wheel. 'Are you saying you approached the guy?'

'Are you saying you're jealous?' Sorcha responded.

Admittedly the idea seemed far-fetched, but why else should he be so uptight?

'Jealous? Huh! I don't deny you're a good-looking girl with a——' Rui broke off to frown. 'Did you approach Mark?' he reiterated.

'No. I was sketching at the harbour this morning and he came over—though I don't see that it matters.'

'It matters. You know why he came over?' Rui demanded as the jeep roared between the wrought-iron gates and into the grounds of Club Marim.

'Because he liked the look of me.'

'No way.'

'Thank you!'

'It was because his father told him to.'

'Why would he do that?' Sorcha asked, puzzled.

He threw her a sideways glance. 'You aren't aware of what Terence Halston does for a living?'

'Haven't a clue.'

Rui was silent for a moment. 'The guy builds timeshare apartments.'

'So?'

'He could be the anonymous client who's angling to acquire your stake in Club Marim.'

'And Mark struck up an acquaintance with the intention of softening me up and making me more receptive to his father's next offer?' she protested. 'Baloney! For a start, how would he know I was Sorcha Riordan?'

'Because Praia do Marim is a small place, and the bank manager could have described you or maybe pointed you out,' Rui said, as though saddled with a not very bright child.

'But Mark never made so much as a passing reference to Club Marim.'

'He didn't ask where you were staying? Surely if you meet someone who's on holiday it's the obvious question.'

Sorcha's brow creased. Now that he mentioned it, the lack of enquiry did seem odd—and hadn't she decided that Mark Halston was an actor? Perhaps he was a better one than she had imagined. 'Mark'll drive you back,' Mr Halston had suggested, but how had he known she needed driving? She could have been staying at the *pension* on the corner of the square, or in a nearby apartment. Sorcha gave her head a little shake. She was letting her imagination run away with her—and so was Rui.

'Mark didn't pick me up with some devious motive in mind,' she declared, 'but even if he had I wouldn't have been hustled into selling my shares to his father behind your back.' She threw him a withering glance. 'I assume that's the reason for your panic?'

'I'm not panicking,' Rui grated. 'But, yes, it's what I was worried about.'

Sorcha felt a lurch of irritation. He had not been jealous. Indeed, the notion of her being seduced by, and interested in, another man had not bothered him one bit. Instead, yet again, the uppermost thought in Rui's mind had been Club Marim. Abruptly she frowned, recalling how he had asked whether she had made the first move.

'You thought I might have made overtures to the Halstons,' she protested, now deeply offended. 'I realise my stepfather did a pretty thorough job of assassinating my character, but I am not—repeat, *not*—underhand. I said I'll sell to the highest bidder and I will. I won't do a private deal with Terence Halston.'

'So you won't see Mark again.'

Sorcha frowned at his profile through the darkness. Was Rui asking—or telling?

'Mark's good fun. He suggested we should go to the disco, and I might,' she declared defiantly, if untruthfully.

'And you might change your mind and enter into negotiations with Terence Halston,' he said.

'No!'

'Why not?' Rui demanded. 'You changed your mind about holding on to your shares.'

Sorcha stared straight ahead. 'That was different.'

'How?'

'It just was. Have you ever considered running a bus service between Club Marim and the village?' she went on, anxious to stop him questioning her further. 'I reckon it'd be a good idea,' she said when he shook his head. 'The walk might not be much in terms of distance but it is hilly, and in the heat it's quite a slog. Some kind of a service would make life easier for visitors who don't have their own transport, plus it could bring in outsiders to use the tennis centre. From what I've seen, there are often free courts, so——'

'You realise Terence Halston's single motivation in life is making money?' Rui interrupted, determinedly returning to his original track. 'If he gained control of Club Marim he'd cover it from boundary to boundary with apartments, and if you'd seen one of his apartments you'd know there isn't enough room inside them to swing a cat.'

Sorcha shone a saccharine smile. 'Why would you want to?' she asked.

He glowered. 'There are times when I'd like to put you across my knee,' he began heatedly, 'and——'

'Violence gets no one anywhere,' she said.

'You're right.' Rui clamped down on his exasperation. 'Maybe I should take a leaf out of

Halston's book and try a little coaxing myself,' he said, as though thinking aloud.

She turned to look at him. 'I beg your pardon?'

'I don't have endless funds and, while I'm prepared to go into debt to stop someone else buying Club Marim and messing it up, obviously there's a limit,' Rui said. 'So if a little seduction could swing things in my favour, why not?'

They were on the road which led up to the cottage, but abruptly he braked, reversed the jeep into the entrance of one of the villas, and set off back down in the opposite direction.

'Where are we going?' Sorcha asked.

'Tonight is the night of the weekly barbecue when we bring in a local band, so I'm taking you dancing.' He turned to give her a slow, sexy smile. 'Beneath the stars. Arms around each other. Two bodies swaying in time to the rhythm.'

Her pulse-rate quickened. Rui might be doing it for effect, yet his smile and the images he was creating were disturbing, none the less.

'I shan't be seeing Mark Halston again and I wasn't seduced, so a charade on your part is totally unnecessary,' Sorcha said hastily.

The corner of his mouth quirked. 'I reckon it's worth a spin.'

'You'll be wasting your time.'

'Wasting my time by dancing with a beautiful girl? Never.'

Sorcha's thoughts dashed every which way. The prospect of being held in his arms again was unnerving. Somehow he must be persuaded to change his mind.

'But if the staff see us together...' she began.

'So there's a bit of talk. It's no reason to go into orbit,' Rui said, quoting her own words back at her.

'I don't want to dance,' she said stubbornly.

'Honey, you'll love it.'

'I'll hate it!'

He spread a large hand on her knee. In a short white dress, Sorcha was bare-legged, and now she stiffened. The touch of his fingers on her skin felt so intimate that it was difficult to keep still.

'You're not frightened of dancing with me, are you?' Rui purred.

'Frightened?' She gave what was intended as a careless trill of laughter. 'I know you think I'm going to spend, spend, spend when I've sold my shares,' Sorcha said, making a wild grab at a diversion, 'but I'm not. In fact, I shan't benefit from the sale at all.'

The barbecue was held at the pool-side, and they had reached the parking area. Taking his hand from her knee, Rui pulled into a space and cut the engine.

'You won't benefit?' he questioned, turning in his seat to frown.

Sorcha wanted to kick herself. Her change of subject had been desperate and ill-considered. She had not only revealed something she had never intended to reveal, but she had also backed herself into the corner of having to reveal even more.

'No. You see, when the proceeds are received I'm going to split them into three,' she said reluctantly, 'and give cheques to Michael and the twins. And if, for some reason, they refuse them, I shall donate the whole amount to charity.'

Rui stared at her. 'Why? I don't follow. Yes, I do,' he said, all of a sudden. 'It's because of Jorge. Because of what I said about him still manipulating you.'

Sorcha's stomach churned. 'I'd rather not continue with this conversation,' she said and, climbing out of the jeep, she set off towards the rhythmic beat of music.

'You're insane!' he declared, striding up alongside. 'What does it matter if the guy still has some tenuous connection? The money will enrich your life and enable you to do all kinds of things you'd never be able to do otherwise.'

They had reached the flagged area which opened up at one end of the pool. Here a small group was playing a sixties rock 'n' roll number, while holidaymakers of all ages flung themselves around in joyful abandon.

'Let's dance,' Sorcha said.

Lacing one hand with hers and placing the other on her waist, Rui twirled her around.

'By off-loading the cash you're being contrary again,' he declared as he pulled her against him. 'And I thought you reckoned you'd grown up.'

Sorcha ignored him. 'You're very good at the jive,' she said as Rui twisted her beneath his arms and executed some neat footwork.

'You should see me do the lambada.'

She raised surprised brows. 'The forbidden dance? You're an expert at that, too?'

'X-rated,' he said, and winked. 'Why are you still so anti-Jorge?' he demanded, switching to his interrogative mode again. 'The only crime he committed was to marry your mother.'

Sorcha's mouth tightened. 'You think so?' she muttered.

Full of apprehension, she waited for his next question, but it did not come, and when he remained silent she gradually began to relax. The music was lively, the beat compulsive, and the two of them moved well together. Sorcha was deciding that dancing at the pool-side was not so bad after all, when the rock 'n' roll session ended and the leader of the group announced the last waltz. As the dreamy strains of a love-song filled the air Rui placed his arms around her, which left her with no alternative than to rest her hands on his shoulders. Sorcha's blood chased through her veins like quicksilver. They were so close that,

when she breathed, she breathed in the clean male
fragrance of his skin. So close that her breasts
were pressed against his chest, and when they
moved her thighs moved against his thighs. She
knew he was deliberately holding her near and
playing the romantic, but did he realise the effect
he had on her?

'No, I don't,' Rui said, all of a sudden.

Horrified, Sorcha looked at him. Surely she
hadn't asked the question out loud?

'Er—sorry?'

'I don't think the only reason you disliked
Jorge was because he married your mother. I
think you also disliked him because he victimised
you. I think that, as you said, he started the
fights, but that, perhaps because he resented your
attachment to your father, he started them because he was determined to be involved with
you—in whatever way he could. And, if it meant
throwing his weight around and being malicious,
that was how it had to be. You may have hated
him, period, but for Jorge the relationship was
love-hate. Love,' Rui stressed.

Sorcha shifted unsteadily beneath his gaze, but
said nothing.

'Have you never thought that in leaving you
your shares Jorge might have been apologising
for his behaviour and trying to make amends?'
he enquired.

She looked somewhere beyond his shoulder. 'Yes.'

'And?'

'And I'm still selling them and still giving away the money.'

Rui swore. 'Sorcha, your stepfather is dead and gone. A past number!' Aware of having raised his voice, he consciously lowered it. 'The guy is history,' he insisted.

Again, Sorcha did not reply.

A few minutes later the waltz came to an end and the musicians bade everyone *boa noite*. As the revellers began to drift away, and the waiters set to work clearing the tables, they returned to the jeep.

'How do you like the cottage?' Rui enquired when they were driving up the hill towards it.

'Very much. It has some lovely views. In fact, I've started a water-colour of the scene as you look from the back garden down the valley to the ocean.' They had arrived, and when he braked the vehicle beside the garden gate Sorcha climbed out. 'Thank you for the lift,' she said.

Rui vaulted out, too. 'I'll see you inside.'

'There's no need,' she protested.

Dancing with him had made her restless and far too aware of him as a virile male, and now all Sorcha wanted was to put some space between them.

'There's every need. After all, you never know if you might meet up with a kidnapper,' he said drily.

She indicated the short paved path which cut across the lawn to the vine-covered front porch. 'Between here and there? I doubt it,' she said, but when she opened the gate he went with her. Unlocking the front door, Sorcha switched on the living-room light. 'See? There's no one lying in wait, no white-slave traffickers, no masked bandits filching the silver.' She took a breath. 'Goodnight.'

Rui stayed where he was, his shoulder resting against the door-jamb. 'You want me to go?'

His brown eyes were hypnotic, and as she looked into them Sorcha felt as if she was drowning in their depths.

'Yes,' she said.

He laughed and, curling an arm around her waist, he drew her to him.

'No, you don't,' he said softly.

Her heart turned a somersault. When Rui tried to be irresistible he was, and he knew it, and he used it. Common sense told her to step away, but, when he bent his head and his mouth found hers, the inertia she felt when he had kissed her before engulfed her again. Closing her eyes, Sorcha wound her arms around his neck and, with her hand pushing into the thick dark hair at the back of his head, she kissed him back.

'Honey,' he murmured, and touched her cheek.

Slowly—agonisingly, maddeningly slowly—Rui trailed his fingers down her throat and across the curves exposed in the scoop neckline of her dress, until they reached the peak of her breast. The breath caught in her throat. She stood rigid. Then, as his fingertips stroked beneath the lace of her bra and across her burgeoning nipple, she started to breathe again. Quickly. Erratically. Beneath his touch, the points of her breasts hardened. Her skin gathered heat. She felt as if she was on fire. In flames. Sorcha drew back. What was happening? Why was her body reacting so violently? Her hormones were not just working overtime, they appeared to have gone haywire.

'This—this is wrong,' she said unsteadily. 'You're supposed to be kissing my fingers.'

Rui looked at her, then his eyes dropped to her parted lips and down to the impassioned rise and fall of her breasts.

'Fingers are all you're offering?' he enquired.

Sorcha nodded.

He gave a wry smile. 'In that case, I'll pass,' he said, and strode off to the jeep.

# CHAPTER SIX

AFTER a night when thoughts of Rui and his caresses had kept her tossing and turning, it was mid-morning before Sorcha awoke. She would not go down to the harbour and sketch, she decided as she ate the usual apple. It was too late. Besides, she was in no mood to see Mark Halston again. Had his father really told him to try and wheedle his way into her favour? she wondered. Whether or not, Praia do Marim would be given a miss for now and, instead, she would spend an hour or two on the beach and later work on her watercolour.

Covering a lime-green swimsuit with a long T-shirt, Sorcha stuffed her sunbathing gear into a bag and set off. She had written a stack of cards which were waiting to be posted, so a detour was taken to the hotel. As she walked into the entrance hall she squared her shoulders. If the gods were kind they would keep Rui from her path, but if they did not she would be the ultimate in nonchalance. She needed to show that his deliberate seduction was not only pointless, but it left her unmoved, though how she could explain away last night's feverish response she did not know.

The postcards were dropped into the mail-box and Sorcha was heading outside again, when footsteps sounded behind her. Despite all her good intentions, she tensed.

'Good morning,' Rui said, coming alongside.

She continued to walk. 'Oh, hello,' she replied, her voice and her smile careless. 'How are you?'

He grimaced. 'I'd be happier if the teacher of the ladies' keep-fit class hadn't just phoned to say she's strained her back. You remember I told you that, in the high season, we run exercise classes as a service for our guests? Well, I'm on my way to advise the ladies who do dance-exercise that today's session has been cancelled.' He sighed. 'I hate it when we let people down.'

'I could run the session,' Sorcha said.

Rui stopped to frown at her. 'You?'

'Yes. The gymnasium I once worked in held aerobics classes, and I learned the routine,' she explained, 'and when their instructor fell ill I substituted for her.' She indicated her bag. 'I was taking my personal stereo down to the beach, so I have a couple of suitable tapes.'

'It's good of you to offer,' he said slowly, 'but——'

'I'd enjoy it. Although I exercise regularly at home, I haven't done here, so I'm in need of a work-out,' Sorcha told him.

Rui gave a sudden grin. 'OK. Let's go over to the sports centre and I'll introduce you.'

The class, which consisted of fifteen or so women, was waiting on one of the squash courts. Most of the participants were in their twenties, though a couple were middle-aged and one looked to be around seventy. When Rui explained that the usual teacher could not be here, but she was an experienced replacement, Sorcha felt a tremor of trepidation. Had her offer been too hasty? It was more than three years since she had taken the aerobics classes, and suppose her memory failed and she ran out of exercises before the stipulated forty-five minutes were up?

She waited until Rui had disappeared, then peeled off her T-shirt and shed her sandals. Inserting a tape into the recorder, she asked the women to take their places on the wooden floor.

'Follow me,' she instructed when the beat began to throb. 'Stretch your arms out sideways and circle your hands. Like this.'

The session started awkwardly. Several of the exercisers had difficulty keeping in time with the music and keeping pace with the different drill. However, movements gradually became more fluent, smiles began to grow, pupils and teacher started to work in harmony. Together they bent and stretched and flexed muscles, and when Sorcha drew the proceedings to a close the women burst into spontaneous applause.

'My husband and I own one of the villas, and as we're both retired we spend several months of the year here,' said the old lady, lingering behind afterwards for a chat. 'I've been attending these classes, off and on, for a long time, and I must tell you that yours was one of the most exhilarating.'

She beamed. 'Thank you.'

'Did you hear that, Mr de Braganca?' the old lady called, and Sorcha swivelled to see Rui strolling on to the court. 'I'm just saying how much I've enjoyed this morning's class.'

'Glad to hear it, Mrs Hutchinson,' he said.

'To be frank, Sorcha here knocks the spots off the usual girl,' she declared, and, with a smiling farewell, she departed.

'See, I have been able to make a contribution to the running of Club Marim,' Sorcha could not resist saying as she towelled a sheen of perspiration from her arms and legs.

Rui grinned. 'Yes, though when you first moved into action I did wonder whether things were going to click.'

Her towelling halted. 'You stayed to check on me?' she demanded.

'No.' He shifted his stance. 'OK, I hung around for a few minutes after the class started, but——'

'You *did* stay to check. You were afraid I was going to make a hash of it, and stayed in case some kind of damage control was required!' she said, her indignation a touch sharper because making a hash of things had been her own fear.

'You don't understand,' Rui began.

'*Au contraire*,' Sorcha said witheringly. 'It's crystal-clear that your mistrust of me is cast in bronze and that, no matter what I do or what I say, nothing is going to change it!' she declared, and, grabbing up her bag, she marched angrily off the court and into the ladies' changing-room.

Sorcha took her time showering and calming down, and when she emerged Rui had gone. As she walked across the trim lawns towards the hotel her face grew pensive. Now that she had helped in one way, a remark Mrs Hutchinson had made prompted her to help in a second more constructive and long-term manner. Though Rui would not consider she was being helpful, she brooded. He would consider she was being plain disruptive! Determination lengthened her stride. As he had said, his views were not the only views, and as of this moment she remained the majority shareholder.

All set to argue her case, Sorcha headed for his office, but when she looked inside the room was empty.

'Rui's over at the conference-centre site,' Izabel told her, appearing along the corridor. 'He could be there for a while.'

'Are José and Antonio around?' Sorcha
enquired.

'Yes. You want to see them?'

'Please.'

It was well past noon before Sorcha left the
suite of offices, and when she came out into the
sunshine she set off back up to the cottage. The
beach would need to be left for another day. She
had work to do.

She made herself a sandwich, then changed
into a black bikini and twisted her hair into a
burnished ash-blonde knot on the top of her
head. Fetching her easel, Sorcha set it up on one
side of the pool. Her brushes and paints were
arranged on an umbrellaed table, and a chair
positioned in the shade. With critical eyes she inspected the work she had already done, then examined the view. The tip of her tongue protruding
between her teeth, she began to mix colours and
add soft organic hues to her landscape.

As the perspiration had dripped during the exercise class, so, in time, it glistened on her skin
again. Sorcha padded barefoot through to the
kitchen to fetch a cold drink. She worked for
another hour, then decided she would have a
swim. At the shallow end of the pool a flight of
semi-circular steps led down into the blessedly
cool water. She submerged herself, then did a
couple of lengths of breast-stroke and a couple
of lengths of lazy crawl.

'Gorgeous,' Sorcha said out loud.

Stripping off her bikini, she tossed it on to the side. She had bathed naked and alone in an isolated bay on a Greek island, and again she wanted to feel the silky caress of water on her body. She swam, floated, burst up and out of the water like a leaping dolphin. A giddiness had taken hold. The exercise class had been a good experience and she was filled with the sheer joy of being alive. Her eyes closed, her face raised to the sun, her arms outspread, she stood motionless, the water lapping at her waist.

'Gorgeous,' Sorcha proclaimed again.

'I agree,' a voice said.

Her eyes flew wide with shock and she saw Rui standing at the far end of the pool. What was he doing here? How long had he been watching? How dared he sneak up unannounced? She did not appreciate his spying on her—*again*—and especially not when she was naked. Sorcha was opening her mouth in protest, when he suddenly began to unfasten the buttons on his shirt. Her mouth fell closed. The protestations died in her throat. Any thought of covering up was stillborn. As if mesmerised, she stared. The shirt was shrugged off his shoulders and dropped to the ground, then Rui bent to remove his shoes and socks. One foot was bared, and the other. Next the wide black leather belt at his waist was unbuckled, and he drew down the zip. Unthreading his legs from his jeans, he kicked them aside. Now the only thing he wore was a pair of skimpy underpants, their pristine white cotton a stark contrast against the sultry gold of his skin. Sorcha's eyes travelled over him. His chest was deep and powerful, his stomach flat, his long legs muscular. He was not particularly hairy. There were dark smudges of hair around the brown circles of his nipples and a line in the centre of his chest which arrowed down across the plain of his stomach to disappear into his briefs. Briefs which were stretched tight and left his manhood in no doubt.

Sorcha gulped in a breath. This striptease, she reminded herself, was yet more of his seduction strategy and should be nonchalantly dismissed. But how? How could she pretend that, with his golden, perfect body, Rui did not resemble a sun god? How could she remain immune to the fact that she was naked, and he nearly so? How could she deny she was becoming aroused? Her breasts pinched. Her heart pumped. Her knees felt weak. Was steam coming off the pool? It should be. Sorcha was bemusedly thinking that if she had been at the deep end she would have drowned, when Rui raised two tanned arms and dived.

Splash! The noise returned her to her senses and shot her into action. As he swam under water she made a grab for her bikini and, almost falling over, managed to wriggle into the briefs. The top

had been yanked on and Sorcha was wildly attempting to fasten the hooks at her back, when
Rui surfaced beside her. Flicking strands of wet
dark hair from his eyes, he placed a hand on her
shoulder and turned her around.

'Let me,' he said.

Sorcha stood like a statue. With her equili-
brium shattered, the last thing she needed was
the intimacy of his dressing her, or to feel the
brush of his fingers against her spine.

'Thank you,' she said primly when he had finished, and, on jelly legs, she walked up the steps
and out of the pool.

'Thank you for rescuing the keep-fit class,' Rui
said, striding out, too. 'I've come to explain why
I stayed to watch at the beginning. It wasn't because I thought you might mess up, it was because——' he hesitated and, as though he could
not help himself, his eyes moved down her
'—because you have one hell of a body and I was
enjoying watching you exercise.'

'You stayed to *ogle*?' Sorcha protested, acutely
aware that she had just been ogling him and now
attempting to remain immune to droplets of water
which were trickling with unnerving sensuality
down the muscled contours of his chest.

'I'm not too keen on the word "ogle", but yes.
And—well, I'm sorry.'

'Sorry you ogled, or sorry I got the wrong
idea?' she enquired.

Rui's mouth curved. 'Sorry you got the wrong idea. The doctor's advised the regular teacher to stay home and rest,' he went on, 'so I also came to see whether you'd be willing to take the class for the next few days? I realise it's a big favour to ask because I know your painting is important, so I'll understand if——'

'I'd be happy to do it,' Sorcha told him.

'Thanks.'

'You're not going to have a proper swim?' she enquired when he sluiced water from his arms.

'I'd like to, but with a meeting arranged in——' Rui inspected his watch '—half an hour there isn't time.' He fixed toffee-brown eyes on hers. 'And, although looking at you had heated me up, all I needed was an opportunity to cool down.'

Sorcha had recovered some of her poise. 'You're cool now?' she said, determinedly holding his gaze.

His mouth curved again. 'As of this moment. And, if I could beg the use of a towel, I'll be dry, too.'

'I'll get one,' she said, and went indoors.

When Sorcha returned she found him studying her landscape.

'I like it,' Rui said as he rubbed himself down. 'It's good.'

She sat on the edge of one of the candy-striped sunbeds. 'It should be even better when it's finished.'

'You're an up-and-coming artist. You can run exercise classes.' Wheeling a second sunbed alongside hers, he sat down and ran a slow fingertip along her arm. 'What else are you a whizz at?'

'Weight training. You never know when you might need to hit someone,' Sorcha said, with a pertinent look at his trespassing finger.

Rui chuckled, then he swung his feet from the ground and stretched out full-length.

She knew she must ignore him and yet, as if lassoed by a rope, her gaze went in his direction. His body was firm, and the muscles which rolled beneath his golden skin were tautly defined.

'Do you exercise?' Sorcha asked.

He shook his head. 'Too busy.'

'Then how do you keep looking so——' quickly 'wonderful' and 'sexy' were rejected '—healthy?' she finally settled on.

'Liposuction,' Rui replied, dead-pan.

She laughed. 'I think you should do a few arms-stretch and knees-bend,' she said.

'Now?' he protested.

'Why not? A work-out never does any harm.' She rose to her feet. 'I'll show you what to do.' When he made no attempt to move, Sorcha tilted her head. 'What's the problem? Is age catching up with you?'

'I'm only thirty-four!'

'Only?' she enquired, opening wide eyes.

Rui clambered from the sunbed. 'Watch this,' he commanded, and proceeded to do twenty sit-ups followed by twenty push-ups.

For someone who reckoned not to take any exercise, he was remarkably supple and strong. Yet as he stood upright, his chest heaving from the exertion, Sorcha gave an impish grin.

'Were you keeping fit—or having one?' she enquired.

'You cheeky little——'

Rui made a grab for her. She was standing beside one of the padded loungers and, as he lunged, she collapsed back on to it. He tickled her and she giggled, and after a minute or two of his chastising and her laughing they ended up with him lying half on top of her. Sorcha felt the weight of his body. She felt his skin, hot and bare against hers. She felt the intimate thrust of his arousal pushing hard against the softness of her thigh.

'Playing these games is not going to work,' she announced in a voice that was painstakingly matter-of-fact.

He scrunched up his brows. 'Games?'

'Acting the big Don Juan, like Mark Halston, won't swing things in your favour. On the contrary, it's swinging them against!'

Rui pushed himself from her and sat up.

'I'm not playing games,' he said.

Sorcha looked at him uncertainly. 'No?'

'Right now, I don't give a damn who gets your shares,' Rui said, and frowned, as though the statement had surprised him. 'All I can think about is making love to you.'

'No!' she said, and this time the word was sharp.

'Sorcha, we only need to touch each other and the earth seems to revolve ten times faster.'

'Not for me,' she claimed hastily.

'For you,' Rui insisted, his intonation firm, and, catching hold of her hand, he raised it to his mouth and slowly began to lick the tips of her fingers one by one.

When Mark Halston had bestowed his extravagant kisses the only thing which had stirred inside her had been distaste, but now... The moist slither of Rui's tongue as he tasted her skin sent darts of desire shooting to her breasts and hurtling down in bitter-sweet spears to strike tantalising and achingly between her thighs.

Sorcha jumped to her feet.

'Nice try,' she said brightly. 'However, moving into overdrive won't——'

'This is for real,' Rui said throatily.

'And nominated for the best actor of the year award is Senhor——'

He gave an impatient sigh. 'Sorcha, I swear that——'

'I presume you haven't spoken to José or Antonio this afternoon?' she enquired.

Rui looked bemused. 'What?'

'You remember I suggested a bus service between here and the village? Well, when I was talking to Mrs Hutchinson——'

'Mrs Hutchinson?' he repeated, struggling to follow this gymnastic leap in the conversation.

'She and her husband can't afford to run a hire-car all the time they're here, and she was complaining about how tiring the walk can be,' Sorcha rattled off. 'I decided to speak to you, but you weren't in your office, and so I went to see José and Antonio and asked them to consider running a bus, maybe three times a day.' She snatched in a breath. 'And now I'd like to call a board meeting to discuss the idea.'

Rui gazed at her in silence for a minute or two, then he sighed. 'There's no need for a meeting,' he said as he walked around the edge of the pool to gather up his clothes. 'I'll organise a bus.'

She smiled. 'Thank you.'

Hooking the towel around his hips, he shed the wet underpants and drew on his jeans. 'That doesn't mean I think it's a fantastic idea. All it

means is that I know who holds the decisive vote,'
he said drily.

'Thanks, all the same. Please could you give
me a lift down to the hotel?' Sorcha asked as he
pulled on his shirt. 'I really ought to go into Praia
do Marim to stock up on food, and if you could
take me that far it would help.'

'Sure,' he agreed, and Sorcha headed inside
the cottage and quickly changed.

'Why don't you eat in the coffee shop or the
restaurant?' Rui enquired when they were driving
down the hill.

'Because if I do it takes an hour minimum,
whereas having my meals at the cottage allows
me to keep on working. And I'm not crazy about
eating alone in public anyway. It'd be useful if
there was a grocery shop at Club Marim,' Sorcha
reflected.

He placed an agonised fist to his brow. 'Spare
me,' he begged.

# CHAPTER SEVEN

THE next few days flew by. Sorcha was busy with the exercise class in the mornings, and spent much of the remainder of the time making friends. Daphne Hutchinson invited her to lunch with her and her husband at their villa, and the old couple were so welcoming that it was late afternoon before she departed. On another occasion, a trio of the younger women asked if she would care to make up a four for tennis, and afterwards insisted on her accompanying them to the beach. Everyone had such a good time that the routine was repeated the following day, and the next. Sorcha was grateful for the activity because it left her little opportunity to think about Rui—though each night, when she went to bed, he filled her mind.

The trouble was, she *did* believe he was genuinely attracted to her, and she was forced to acknowledge that the feeling was mutual. But where did they go from there? she brooded as, once again, she lay awake until the early hours. The answer could only be—nowhere. Sorcha stared into the darkness. Rui had said he wanted to make love to her but, in addition to her reluc-

131

tance to embark on what presumably would be a glorified holiday romance, there was another consideration. He would bring all his Latin verve and intensity to their intimacy and would expect—demand—equal passion from his partner. She was unable to supply that passion, she thought bleakly. If they made love her limitations would be brutally exposed and he would be disappointed—and she could not bear that.

After several days when she had not put brush to paper the urge to paint grew, and the next morning Sorcha rose early. The aerobics class did not start until eleven, and if she worked hard there was a chance her landscape could be completed. Clad in her swimsuit and with her straw hat shading her eyes, she sat at the easel. As the sun rose in the sky Sorcha deftly applied colour, sharpened lines, blurred edges. She was evaluating the picture as a whole, when the noise of a braking vehicle suddenly intruded into her consciousness.

'Oh, no!' she yelped in alarm.

When she painted she often lost track of time, but it couldn't be eleven o'clock *already*. Desperately Sorcha searched around for her watch. Her wrist had become sweaty in the heat and she had taken it off, but where was it now?

'I'm so sorry,' she gabbled as Rui appeared around the side of the cottage. She slid her feet into her sandals. Hauled on her shirt. 'I never intended to be late for the class and——'

'You're not. It's only ten-thirty. Though I've come to tell you that the regular woman's rung to say she'll be reporting for duty this morning, so your services are no longer required.' After thanking her again for taking over, Rui gestured towards her painting. 'How's it progressing?'

'It's finished——' Sorcha hesitated '—unless I decide to deepen the colour of the sky.'

He walked forward to make an inspection. 'The sky looks fine to me.'

Her lower lip caught between her teeth, she studied the landscape again. 'It is,' she decided.

'So now you're free to have a cold drink or a cup of coffee,' Rui said with a grin.

'It'll be a coffee,' she said, and paused. 'There's something I want to say.'

'Then I'll have a coffee, too. If that's OK?'

Telling him she had something to say had not been an invitation for him to linger, Sorcha thought uneasily—though, knowing the pace Rui set for himself, he would not linger for long.

She flashed a smile. 'Of course. You take it black, with one sugar?' she checked, recalling the night they had dined together.

'Please.'

In the kitchen she made two mugs of instant coffee, then returned to the patio, where she joined him at the umbrellaed table.

'Now that I know more about Club Marim,' Sorcha said when she had taken a sip, 'I realise what a disaster it'd be to let someone like Terence Halston get their hands on it—and so I accept your last offer.'

Rui's dark brows lowered. 'This is an overnight decision?' he enquired.

'No. It's the result of several days' thinking. I've been listening to what the people who stay here say,' she explained. 'How fond they are of the place and how much they appreciate the care with which it's run. It's obvious that if it all fell apart they'd be most upset.'

'But it might not fall apart because the anonymous bidder may *not* be Halston,' he said. 'It could be a reasonable firm who will——'

'Your offer is accepted,' Sorcha insisted. 'Rui, everything that has happened here is thanks to you, and it's only right and proper that *you* should see Club Marim through to its completion and beyond.'

He smiled. 'Thank you.'

'Can you give me an idea of how long it'll take you to complete the sale?' she asked.

'I'll need a while to cash in my investments, but I reckon...roughly four to five weeks.' Rui swallowed a mouthful of coffee, then set down his mug. 'You and I may have started off badly,' he said, 'but——'

'"All's well that ends well"',' Sorcha quoted merrily.

'Who says it's ended?' he enquired, gazing at her with steady brown eyes.

Her heart turned over. Why did he have to look at her like that? Why must he make her feel so *torn*? One half of her was tempted to throw caution to the winds, smile encouragingly, and take the chance that if—when—they reached lovemaking she could fake her way through. But the other half knew she would be inviting disaster.

Sorcha pushed back the chair and stood up. 'I'd better go down to Praia do Marim and advise the bank manager that my shares are no longer available,' she declared.

'No need,' Rui said. 'I can phone him from my office.'

'Would you? Thanks. Perhaps you could go and do it now,' she suggested.

'OK,' he agreed, and swallowed down the rest of his coffee, 'but I'll be straight back.'

Dismay fluttered through her. 'You're coming back?' she enquired.

He nodded. 'There's something I want to say to you. I've called round several times hoping to talk, but you were always out.'

What did Rui want to talk about—them? It seemed a distinct possibility. Sorcha eyed him warily from beneath the brim of her hat. While his heavy work-load was restrictive, she had decided that his failure to make contact over the past few days had been because he had given up on the idea of their becoming involved. But—of course—Rui was not the kind who gave up easily.

'You have a busy schedule and—and talking takes time,' she protested.

'So I'll make time. In fact, I shall take the day off,' Rui declared, with the air of someone reaching a momentous decision. 'I'll go and ring the bank manager and I'll let Izabel know I'm off duty, and while I'm gone perhaps you could make us another cup of coffee?'

'Er—yes,' she said.

When he disappeared Sorcha began clearing away her painting tackle. Fretfully she chewed at her lip. The prospect of listening to whatever it was Rui had to say on his return filled her with misgivings, but would he return—or might he be side-tracked by some matter which *demanded* his attention? As she rinsed out her brushes Sorcha sent up a fervent prayer. Please let a crisis arise. Please let him be inextricably tied up. On tenterhooks, she waited. Fifteen minutes ticked by, and twenty, but he did not reappear. When he had been gone half an hour she gave a relieved sigh. Rui's taking a day off belonged to the realms of fantasy. Abruptly she frowned. Wasn't that the sound of the jeep coming up the lane?

'You thought I'd got involved in work?' Rui enquired, arriving to find her hastily plugging in the kettle. He placed a large cardboard box on the table. 'This is the reason for the delay. I called in at the coffee shop and asked them to provide a carry-out lunch, so we have egg mayonnaise, salad, cold meats, chocolate mousse—your favourite,' he grinned, 'and a bottle of wine. Shall I put everything in the fridge?'

Sorcha summoned up a smile. 'Please. Did you speak to the bank manager?' she asked.

'Yes. He says he'll pass on the message, and that as his client's kept you waiting for so long he's in no position to complain. And when I made a remark about how your stake might have appealed to Terence Halston, he was very quick to agree.'

'So you think his client was Halston?'

'Definitely.' Rui wiped a slick of sweat from his brow. 'It must be in the eighties outside, so suppose we stay indoors and have a glass of wine instead of coffee?'

'Fine,' she agreed.

'What I wanted to talk about is my so-called seduction,' he began when they were seated in the relative cool of the white-walled living-room. He frowned. 'I said it was to try and coax you to accept my offer for your shares—and for a while I told myself that, too—but the shares didn't feature and it was an excuse.'

'For what?' she queried.

His brown eyes met hers. 'To be able to touch you, to kiss you.'

Like a ball in a pinball machine, Sorcha ricocheted from delight to despair and back again. 'Oh,' she said.

'I guess I'd better begin at the beginning,' Rui reflected, tasting his wine. 'After you left here in April I decided I'd prefer it if we never met again, yet while you were gone I doubt ten consecutive minutes went by without my thinking about you. Then, when you arrived and steered clear of me, I felt . . . cut.'

'I steered clear because you were so stiff and starchy,' she told him.

'I realise that, but at the time I was damned if I'd admit you'd bewitched me and so whenever we met it wound me up.' He gave a wry smile. 'However, I swiftly decided that keeping a distance suited me, too, only the next thing I knew I was using Mark Halston as a means of getting closer by pretending to seduce you.' He cast her a look from beneath his dark lashes. 'You were right about my being jealous. When I saw young Halston slavering over you I wanted to murder the little jerk! Yet it still took time for it to dawn on me that, as in Club Marim I'd found the right career, so in you I'd found the right woman.'

Delight and despair vied within her again. 'The right woman?' Sorcha echoed.

He nodded. 'Remember I said that when we met I knew you'd screw things up for me? You have—emotionally. You see, I'd decided there was no way I'd become involved in any kind of serious relationship until Club Marim was complete. Are you dating someone?' he demanded.

'No,' she said, startled by the sudden question.

'Then why the frown? OK, it's early days and, heaven knows, I don't intend to push, but I get the impression you care for me, too.' Rui's lips curved. 'Just a bit?'

Her mind a tangle of emotions, Sorcha looked at him. If he had been promoting a holiday romance it would have been easy to turn him down. But now... Her heart raced. Now she was tempted to confess that she did care, and more than a bit. Dared she? Dared she let their relationship develop?

'What makes you feel so strongly about Club Marim that you've allowed it to dominate your life?' Sorcha enquired, needing to gain some time.

'It's the fact that until I came here I'd never stuck at a job, a decent job, and making a success of this one seemed as if it was my last chance.'

She stared at him along the length of the sofa. 'You'd never stuck at a job?' she repeated incredulously.

Rui shook his head. 'If you recall, I once told you how Jorge felt we had something in common.

Well, the common ground was that we were both the youngest sons in wealthy families who, from birth, had been expected to join the family business.' He frowned. 'We were both also the youngest sons by several years, and indulged and spoiled sons. Sons who lacked ambition.'

'You're ambitious,' Sorcha protested.

'I am now. Maybe too much so,' he remarked, with a dry smile. 'Yet for years I drifted and I could have become a parasite—like Jorge.'

'He admitted he was a parasite?' she enquired curiously.

'No! According to him, he was a driving force in Almeida Wine, though his sloth when he was here made it clear he had little interest in business. He didn't confess to having been spoiled rotten, either. But he did say that having older brothers—hard-working brothers—meant you had a hell of a lot to live up to.'

'Does your family also produce wine?' she enquired.

Rui shook his head. 'They own a civil-engineering company, which specialises in the construction of power stations world-wide. De Braganca Limitada was founded by my great-grandfather, and, since my father's retirement a couple of years ago, has been run by my two brothers. It was always intended that I'd join them there but, despite getting a degree in business management, when the time came I said no.'

'Why?' Sorcha asked.

He fingered his lower lip. 'The honest answer is, I don't know,' he said thoughtfully. 'Though I suspect it could have been because I sensed that, if I became part of the family set-up, I'd never amount to anything much. That I'd always be regarded as the baby, treated as the baby, and thus would be tempted to *act* like the baby. Because it had been pre-ordained, my refusal to join De Braganca created all kinds of fuss,' he said in rueful remembrance. 'However, eventually my father realised I didn't intend to change my mind and he rang round his contacts, who came up with a number of jobs—which I proceeded to work my way through, never staying longer than a few months.'

'Perhaps you didn't stay because you resented your father's fixing them for you,' she suggested.

'Possibly,' Rui agreed, 'though I never made much of an effort to find employment for myself. I had the vague idea that one day I'd become a business tycoon and wow everyone, but at that time a career didn't excite me.'

'What did?'

He grinned. 'Driving fast cars, riding fast horses, getting on close terms with women—fast and otherwise. My job-hopping lasted for a couple of years, with my family growing increas-

ingly annoyed,' he continued, 'then I decided I
wanted to see more of the world. Because he felt
sure I'd settle down at the end of it, my father
sent me off with his blessing. I went to Nepal,
where I toyed with the idea of becoming a
Buddhist, hitch-hiked around Thailand, visited
the Australian outback.' Rui gave a nostalgic
smile. 'It was a great experience, but, when the
time came for me to start on a career back at
home, again I wasn't interested. I went through
a succession of dead-end jobs, then, after a
mammoth row when my father informed me I
was heading nowhere and fast, I took off for the
States.'

Sorcha looked at him over the rim of her glass.
'Without your father's blessing?'

'With his boot up my ass,' he said pungently.
'He also managed to restrict my access to a fair
amount of my capital—thank the lord, because
I was spending it at a rate of knots—and so, like
you——' he smiled at her '—I took whatever work
was going.'

'For example?' she asked, fascinated.

'I pumped gas, drove a cab, did all kinds of
labouring jobs on building sites. Eventually I
wound up as a factory hand in California, where
I stayed for two years. Then one day I realised I
was fed-up to the back teeth with the job, with
the girl I was living with, and with myself. So I
returned to Portugal—and my father's condem-

nation. Before I'd convinced myself that his remarks about my being a loser were so much
baloney, but by now I was approaching thirty. I
only had to look around and see how well my
contemporaries were doing in their careers,
and——' Rui raised and lowered his shoulders
'—it didn't do much for my ego. Again my father
suggested I should join him and my brothers, but
again I refused. I needed to refocus my life, yet
I had no idea what I wanted to do. All I knew
was that I had to do it on my own and that, if I
was ever to hold my head up high, it was essential I make a go of it!'

'You sound to have become desperate,' Sorcha
observed.

'I was. I despatched endless applications for
jobs in everything from advertising to consul-
tancy work, but without any training or experience it was inevitable that all I received was
"thanks, but no, thanks". Then, by chance, I saw
an advertisement for a manager for Club
Marim——' he swallowed a mouthful of wine
'—but when I came for an interview and was offered the position I didn't know whether to accept
it or not. The development wasn't much of a development and the job didn't seem much of a
job. Virtually all it amounted to was being a
caretaker.'

'I don't imagine Jorge seemed much of an employer, either,' Sorcha said pithily.

'His indifference came over loud and clear,' Rui agreed. 'However, I recognised that Club Marim possessed potential.'

'Which you soon set about developing?'

He nodded. 'Much to my father's astonishment, I became one of the world's aspirers and achievement orientated, and Jorge obliged by going along with everything I suggested. Thank heavens, because if I hadn't come good here——'

'You'd have come good somewhere else,' she said firmly.

'Would I? Maybe, but Jorge gave me the chance, for which I'm eternally grateful, and that's why when he demonstrated a desire to talk about you I felt duty-bound to listen.' Rui moved closer along the sofa. 'Forgive me?'

Sorcha smiled. 'You're forgiven.'

'So, now that that's all cleared up, how about us?' he enquired.

For the past few minutes she had been relaxed, but now her nerves twitched and juddered.

'Wh-what about us?' she said unsteadily.

Raising his hand, Rui drew his knuckle tenderly down the smoothness of her cheek. 'Sorcha, every time I see you now I see you standing naked in the pool. And I want you. Lord, how I want you. And you want me, too,' he said softly.

Although his statement was not a question, there was a moment when she could have erected some kind of a defence. She did not. Instead, entranced by the touch of his fingers and the tone of his voice, she gazed at him. Sorcha recognised the hunger which burned in his eyes, and felt an echoing need ripple through her. It was a need which obliterated all doubts and fears.

Taking her wine glass from her, Rui placed it with his on the low table, then his arms slid around her. The first brush of his lips was gentle, but then his mouth opened on hers and he began kissing her with deep, impassioned kisses. Sorcha's blood tingled. Her breathing quickened. She pressed closer, revelling in the hard strength of his body. He was right, she thought dimly, all it needed was for them to touch and the world did spin faster. And if it spun quickly enough . . .

Desperately she began to tug at the buttons on his shirt.

'You'll pull them off,' Rui warned against her mouth.

'I don't care.'

He drew back to smile, delighted that her earlier hesitancy had dissolved and she was now as eager for them to make love as he.

'But I don't want to have to sew them back on again,' he said, 'so let me help you.'

Together they unfastened his shirt and Rui stripped it away in one fluid, economical movement. Her gaze concentrated on him, Sorcha marvelled at the sheen of his skin and the male beauty of his torso. A need to touch exploded inside her and, lifting her hands, she drew her palms down from the width of his shoulders and slowly across his chest, her fingers trailing over his nipples. Rui shuddered convulsively.

'I want to look at you, to touch you,' he murmured, and he drew her shirt from her, tossing it to the floor, where it landed with a soft thud. Adroitly he unhooked the straps from her shoulders and eased her swimsuit down. 'You have beautiful breasts,' he said thickly as their creamy fullness and swollen dark-rose points were exposed to his piercing gaze. 'So round, so firm——' he stroked languorous fingers over the naked globes '—so silky.'

As he lowered his head and kissed her nipples Sorcha felt an intense spasm of pleasure. A shivering joy. Steering her back against the softness of the cushions, Rui bent, and, fastening his mouth over a rigid peak, he began to suck. This was no young lover's tentative caress, she acknowledged mutely as wave after wave of pleasure began to shudder wildly through her body. This was a grown man, expertly giving—and taking—pleasure. Wonderingly she opened her eyes and saw the coarse darkness of his head against the pale honey of her breast. Thrusting her hand into his hair, Sorcha curled it possessively around her fingers, drawing him closer as she gave herself up to the thrilling sensations which he was inspiring.

When Rui finally raised his head he was breathing heavily.

'Dear God, *Sorcha*,' he groaned as his hand possessed the aroused skin which remained moist from the attentions of his mouth, then he leaned over to capture her other breast.

As he feasted on her she twisted and arched towards him, glorying in the tormenting lap of his tongue and the graze of his teeth. She had never known it was possible to feel so giddy with desire, so uninhibited, so in need. When Rui released her the second time Sorcha clutched at his shoulders and rubbed against him, dragging her nipples against his chest until he shuddered again.

'You're a witch. A beautiful, tantalising witch,' he said, and, catching hold of her hand, he drew it down between their bodies until she felt the pulsing jut of his maleness beneath the tight denim of his jeans. 'I want to see your face at the moment when I enter you,' he muttered, his voice ragged and raw. 'At the moment when I take you.'

Panic flared in a thin piercing flame. This far everything had been wonderful, but suppose when their lovemaking reached its climax she felt nothing? Rui was too astute and too experienced to be fooled.

'What's wrong?' he asked, suddenly drawing back.

Sorcha shone a smile. To succumb to an attack of the jitters was sheer foolishness. Everything would continue to be wonderful—wouldn't it?

'Nothing,' she said.

He took a controlling breath. 'Sorcha, I'm sure about my feelings, but you must be sure, too.'

'I am,' she said quickly.

'So why withdraw just then? OK, it was an internal thing, but you were thinking about something and...hesitating.' Rui took another breath. 'This isn't all just a game, is it?' he demanded.

'A game?' she queried in bewilderment.

'You're not getting back at me for supposedly seducing you? You didn't set out to go so far and then just—just stop?' His mouth twisted slightly and she saw how hurt he was. 'For pity's sake, how can you do that?'

'I haven't. I'm not,' Sorcha protested, alarmed to discover that his alertness meant he had detected her apprehension.

'So what's the matter?'

'Nothing,' she said, and gave another smile.

Rui reached for his shirt. 'There's a name for women like you,' he said bitterly as he pulled it on. 'Women who deliberately arouse——'

Sorcha hooked up the straps of her swimsuit. 'You were arousing me, too,' she defended.

'I was involved in what is commonly called foreplay,' he said in brusque, clipped tones, 'which means *before* making love, which was my intention. But you never intended us to make love.'

'I did!' she wailed.

'Then explain your withdrawal. Or are you going into your Iron Curtain mode again?' Rui asked scathingly.

She frowned. 'I don't know what you mean.'

'No? It's noticeable that on certain occasions—as, for example, when the conversation gets around to your stepfather—you either say the minimum or you announce that it's a no-go area and you don't want to talk about it.' With angry fingers he started to fasten his shirt. 'And, if you've decided you're not talking now, I might as well leave.'

As he rose to his feet Sorcha's insides cramped. The intimacy she had craved might be over, but she could not allow him to walk away. She could not let Rui believe he had been tricked. She had to say something—she cast him a glance—and that something would need to be the truth.

'I—I was thinking that, if I needed to pretend I was ... ecstatic, you would know.'

'Why would you need to pretend?' he demanded.

'Because——' her face clouded '—I don't usually enjoy lovemaking.'

Rui gave a curt laugh of disbelief. 'You'll have to do better than that.'

'I'm cold,' Sorcha insisted. 'Frigid.'

'What a load of...rubbish!' he protested.

'I am.'

'You appear to forget that I've seen you revelling in the sensual feel of water and the heat of the sun on your naked body. You also forget that, minutes ago, you were damn near tearing off my shirt,' he said, his voice harsh with scorn.

'Maybe, but——'

'You think I can't recognise a highly sexual woman when I see one? You think I don't know that if we'd made love you would have given yourself to me with total abandon? OK, you reckon you're frigid,' he said impatiently when she frowned. 'Why?'

'It—it's because of something that happened to me when I was young,' Sorcha said, and to her dismay she felt the sharp sting of tears.

Rui paused between one shirt button and the next to peer at her.

'You're crying,' he said.

'No,' she claimed, and hurriedly blinked the tears away.

He came to sit down beside her on the sofa. 'Sorcha, I want to know what this is all about,' he said, his voice gentle now. He stroked her wrist. 'Please.'

She bowed her head. In telling him the truth, she had not intended to reveal the whole truth. But his tenderness wrapped itself around her heart and weakened that intention.

'It was Jorge,' she began, and stopped. Her throat had gone dry. There was a pain along her jaw.

'Jorge?' Rui queried.

The tears which had stung were brimming. 'The reason I've never enjoyed sex is because— because he molested me.'

# CHAPTER EIGHT

'GOD almighty, *no*!' Rui protested. His hand closed protectively around hers. 'When did this happen?'

'When—when I was twelve,' Sorcha told him, the words emerging taut and jerky.

'Jorge raped you?'

She shook her head. 'Before things could get that far I managed to throw a glass of water into his face, and escape and lock myself in the bathroom. But for years afterwards I was terrified he might try again.'

'The bastard!' Rui said viciously.

'When I grew older I realised I mustn't let the incident ruin my life, so I tried hard to put it behind me...and work my feelings through...and not develop any kind of hang-up. Mostly, I've succeeded. I mean, I haven't become a man-hater...and I'm not a virgin.' Sorcha attempted a smile. 'Alabaster or otherwise. But whenever I've made love before it's—it's been as though I'm wearing a mental chastity belt and I can't let it go.'

'If it was in my power to change what Jorge did, lord knows, I would, but—I'm sorry, so very,

very sorry,' Rui said, and when she looked into his face she saw that his eyes, too, were glistening.

Up until now she had had a hold on her emotions, albeit fragile, but to see her own anguish mirrored in his face snapped that hold. With a shuddering sob, Sorcha laid her head on his shoulder and began to cry. She had been deceiving herself, she thought as the tears streamed down her face. She had not come to terms with Jorge's assault. Not properly. All she had done was push the hurt and fear away into a broom cupboard in her mind, where they had lived on through the years, denied yet festering. But now that cupboard had been opened.

Rui held her close and stroked her hair and whispered comforting words, but it was a long time before she finally reached for a box of tissues and blew her nose.

'I must look a mess,' Sorcha said.

Wryly he eyed the mascara that puddled her cheeks.

'Yes.'

'You're supposed to say I look beautiful,' she demurred.

'A mess *and* beautiful.'

'And the age of gallantry is reckoned to be dead,' Sorcha said wryly.

Rui smiled, but swiftly sobered. 'Who else knows about this?' he enquired.

'Only you.'

A line etched itself between his brows. 'Your mother isn't aware of what happened?'

'No. I did wonder whether I should tell her after Jorge died. It would have explained a lot. But I couldn't see the point of causing her yet more distress, and all I wanted to do was forget about it. Some hope,' Sorcha muttered. 'When Jorge was alive I'd disciplined myself so that I only thought about him when we met, then he was banished until the next time. Yet since his death I seem to have been plagued with memories,' she said, and fell silent.

'I realise you were a child while Jorge was an adult and thus in a position of authority,' Rui said, 'but if you'd told your mother at the time——'

'I tried to, but she wouldn't believe me. She maintained he was being friendly, that was all.'

'But if you'd spelled it out——'

'It was a difficult situation,' Sorcha protested. 'As far as Mum was concerned, Jorge was the answer to all her prayers. Before she'd been forever anxious, but after she became his wife she was calm, relaxed, contented. So, I was frightened of shattering that contentment and of damaging their relationship. Also I . . . I——' She fumbled to a halt. Should she tell Rui the other reason why she had failed to insist that her mother must listen? The predominant reason? Sorcha gazed down at the crumpled tissue she held in her hand. But what would he think of her if she did? Would his sympathy vanish—to be replaced by disgust? 'I was scared of wrecking my mother's marriage,' she repeated.

'The marriage she went into because she wanted financial security.'

Her head jerked up. 'Jorge admitted that?' she asked in surprise.

Rui nodded. 'His relationship with your mother seems to have been the one area where he was completely honest—though he was only honest because he felt he had to be.'

'Meaning?'

'The frequency of his visits to Portugal had nothing to do with Club Marim and everything to do with chasing other women.' He cast her a searching glance. 'Are you surprised?'

Sorcha thought for a moment. 'No. Although Jorge was fond of my mother, his feelings for her could never be described as a grand passion, and he was continually chatting up some female or other.' She hesitated. 'Presumably that was why he never brought Mum and the twins to the Algarve?'

'Yes. When he was here he considered himself to be a bachelor and wasn't too discreet, and someone could have talked. Although I was aware of his philandering, I didn't feel it was my place to comment,' Rui continued, 'but Jorge picked up on my disapproval. So, with the intention of excusing himself, I guess, he told me how your mother had married him for his money—and how he'd married her to pacify his brothers.'

'His brothers? Why did he need to pacify them?' Sorcha asked, puzzled.

'It seems they'd grown weary of his having one five-minute affair after another with women who became successively younger as he grew older, and had issued an ultimatum. They said that if he didn't settle down with someone suitable he'd be ousted from Almeida Wine and left to make his own way in the world. Puts a new slant on things, doesn't it?' Rui said drily as she looked at him with surprised eyes.

'And how.'

'Talking about wine, would you care for a refill?' he asked.

Sorcha nodded. 'Please.'

'I assume that, as your mother worked as Jorge's secretary before they were married, she must have been aware of his reputation?' he said when he had topped up their glasses.

'She knew he liked the ladies,' Sorcha acknowledged, then grew pensive. 'She might have also guessed he was playing around afterwards. When I asked her about Club Marim she was dismissive. She appeared to regard his involvement as...something which kept him happy, but something which didn't concern her and which she had absolutely no wish to be concerned with.'

'So long as Jorge provided a comfortable life-style, she was willing to accept his infidelities?' He grimaced. 'Not my idea of how a marriage should be.'

'Nor mine, but after my father walked out my mother's priorities seemed to have changed. Love was no longer the be-all and end-all; instead the major requirement of any husband was that he should offer financial stability.' Sorcha paused. 'I don't mean she craved money for money's sake, but she craved the protection and security it can bring.'

'The breakdown of a marriage is always traumatic, but she appears to have taken your father's desertion particularly hard,' Rui remarked.

'Yes, but, you see, she was still in love with him and she knew he still loved her.'

He looked perplexed. 'Then why the split?'

'Because Dad was unhappy with the direction his life was taking and wanted to make changes, whereas Mum had settled snugly into being a housewife and mother, and was appalled by the idea of disruption.' Sorcha drank from her glass. 'My father had a well-paid job with a firm of estate agents, but selling property had never interested him,' she explained. 'He's told me that eventually he realised life isn't a dress rehearsal and if you're not satisfied then it's up to you to do something about it; so he decided to enrol at college and study sculpture. He'd wanted to do that when he'd left school, but his parents had rubbished the idea. So had my mother,' she said, with a sigh. 'Dad explained how he could apply for a grant and that, although there'd be less money, if he took evening work they could manage, but Mum was horrified. He insisted he'd reached the head-banging stage and that if he was to stay sane he *had* to give sculpting a try, but she refused to take any notice. So one day, after she'd begun to talk about how much she wanted to have another child, he packed his bags and departed.'

'How old were you?'

'Six, and Michael was eight. Dad's leaving was hard enough for us, but it devastated my mother.'

'If they loved each other, surely they could have worked something out?' Rui protested.

'You'd think so. Dad could have offered to limit the sculpting experiment to a year and Mum could have said she'd help by working part-time, too, but neither of them seems to have been willing to compromise,' Sorcha said sorrowfully. 'Although she had her fair share of admirers, it was years before my mother so much as glanced at another man,' she continued. 'But then she went to work for the Almeida Wine Company, and for Jorge.'

'Who, a few months earlier, had received instructions to find himself a wife—a mature one.'

She gave a wry smile. 'Mum's timing was just right.'

'And Jorge must have seemed tailor-made as a second husband.'

'Ideal,' Sorcha agreed. 'He could provide financial security, and he didn't mind taking on two kids. Plus he wanted to start a family of his own.'

'In order to demonstrate his credentials as the solid family man to his brothers,' Rui said astringently. 'And your mother was longing to pack in being a secretary and have more babies?'

'Had been for ages. But, whereas there'd been no trouble during her pregnancies with Michael and me, this time, despite conceiving with remarkable regularity, she seemed destined to miscarry.' A nerve jumped in Sorcha's temple. 'It wasn't long before she began spending days, weeks and, in time, months in hospital.'

'Which is when Jorge made his move?'

She stared down at the wine in her glass. Although she had known it was inevitable they would return to the subject, over the last few minutes her tension had lessened, but now a steel band seemed to be tightening around her chest, making her feel choked and cramped inside.

'Yes.'

'Tell me about it. It won't be easy for you,' Rui said gently, 'but I need to know.'

Her chin tilted. 'I'm OK. When my mother first went into hospital I gradually became aware of a change in Jorge's attitude towards me. Until then he'd kept his distance, but now he seemed to be forever hugging me or tickling me or pulling me down on to his knee. It was done in a jokey way and yet, somehow, it felt creepy. However, I decided I must be imagining it. What no one remembers now is that, at the beginning, I liked Jorge,' Sorcha explained. 'There might have been a bond with my father, but by marrying my mother Jorge had made her happy, so I was happy, too. And, after years of it just being the three of us, it felt good to have a man around. Also we'd moved into a bigger house, and Jorge was paying for Mike and me to have riding lessons, and he'd tell us jokes, and—well, in so many ways life was cheerier and much fuller than before.' Her face clouded. 'But one evening when Mum was away he crept into my bedroom. Although he'd never done it before, he reckoned he'd come in to kiss me goodnight, but then——' She shuddered.

'You can skip the details,' Rui murmured.

She gave a bleak smile. 'Thanks, I will. When I protested Jorge insisted that by allowing him to cuddle me earlier I'd been tempting him and, although I felt confused about it at the time, later I was forced to accept that he was right. I mean, I hadn't stopped him and so what happened could be said to have been partly my fault.' Her fingers tightened around the stem of her glass, the blood draining from them. 'That's why I didn't try too hard to tell my mother. That's why I—I *couldn't*.'

Rui removed the glass from her trembling fingers and put it aside. 'You were a young girl, innocent and suggestible,' he said firmly, 'and when Jorge—who was a man of over forty, dammit!—talked about being tempted he was plausibly and very craftily shifting the blame. And ensuring you'd keep quiet. I assume your distress was responsible for your being expelled from school?' he continued.

Sorcha bobbed her head. 'All I could think about was what Jorge had done, and the fear and the dread made me aggressive. So, when the teachers complained that I was showing no interest in lessons and had stopped handing in homework, I told them I didn't give a damn.'

'Which must have gone down well,' he remarked drily. 'And then you demanded to go to boarding-school with the hope of evading him?'

'Yes. I felt safe, until——' the nerve jumped again in her temple '—a holiday coincided with my mother's being admitted to hospital for some tests. Then I was terrified, wondering whether, in her absence, Jorge might pounce again.'

Rui frowned at her tense expression. 'And he did?'

'Yes, the very first night he sneaked into my bedroom. When he came through the door I almost died of fright. However, I plucked up the courage and informed him that if he laid so much as a finger on me not only would I yell blue murder and waken Mike—who, because he sleeps like a log, had slept through everything the first time—but I'd also inform the police.'

'And Jorge exited?'

'Reluctantly. However, when I went back to school I was so unstrung I had to hit out in some way, so I did the most scandalous thing I could think of—I smoked.'

'And ensured you were caught?'

'That was an integral part,' Sorcha acknowledged.

'You were making a cry for help,' Rui said.

She nodded. 'I think at the back of my mind was the hope that if I was naughty enough someone would demand to know why, though they never did,' Sorcha said ruefully. 'I also think I was attempting to punish Jorge and my mother. Anything that I knew would cause them offence, I did. Any rules they made, I broke. Anything they declared was off limits, I immediately became involved in.' She sighed. 'And, once I started behaving badly, it was like being on a runaway train.'

'You feel your mother failed you?' he enquired.

'Yes,' Sorcha said simply. 'She must have realised my change of character was connected with Jorge, but she chose to believe the tale he spread; that my waywardness was simply resentment at his replacing my father. I know human beings don't enjoy having to face the unpalatable, but she never asked the obvious questions, presumably because she was afraid of the answers.' Her hands moved in an aimless gesture. 'I'm not saying my mother knew what had happened, what I'm saying is that it suited her not to know. As it suited her not to know about Jorge's extramarital activities.'

'Yet you and she appear to be on good terms,' Rui observed.

'We are, and since Jorge died our relationship has become easier. But for many years there was a chasm between us, and I doubt it'll ever completely disappear.' Sorcha was silent and brooding for a moment. 'I don't know whether his own daughters would have been in any danger, but I'd decided that if the twins were girls I would tell my mother what Jorge had done—despite my being in some way resonsible.'

'Sorcha, you have nothing to reproach yourself for, *nothing*!' Rui said forcibly. 'You said you told him you'd inform the police,' he went on. 'That's what the girl he assaulted here threatened.'

Wide-eyed, she gazed at him. 'Jorge assaulted some—someone on the Algarve?' she faltered.

'The sixteen-year-old daughter of one of Izabel's neighbours.'

'So that's why she disliked him.'

'Disliked? Izabel would have strung the guy up from the nearest tree if she'd had her way,' Rui said bitingly. 'But when the girl protested Jorge told her what he'd told you, that she'd deliberately tempted him. Which, of course, she hadn't—as *you* hadn't,' he insisted.

Sorcha looked into the brown eyes that were so resolute, so sure. For more than a decade she had believed that, no matter how unwittingly, some of the blame for being molested must lie with her. But now...

'However, this time his victim was older and he wasn't married to her mother,' Rui continued, 'so she immediately said she would report him to the authorities. Yet again Jorge made a reluctant exit.'

'And did the girl report him?' she asked.

'No. She's the shy, timid type and she couldn't face the embarrassment. Her parents realised something had gone wrong, but it was a couple of months before she could bring herself to tell them—by which time Jorge had died.' He gave a twisted smile. 'Apparently she'd withdrawn into herself, but I reckon your lust for outrage was a darn sight healthier.'

'Probably,' Sorcha agreed. 'Mind you, for years afterwards I felt bitter, until I realised that bitterness is a negative force. I also realised that, although my bad behaviour caused other people all kinds of angst, it was self-destructive because the only person it really damaged was *me*.'

'At which point the demure Miss Riordan was reborn?' Rui enquired drily.

She grinned. 'I don't think I've ever been demure.'

'Neither do I.'

'But I do think,' Sorcha went on slowly, 'that I could be mistaken in believing I was at fault.'

'I don't think you're mistaken, I *know* it,' Rui declared.

She looked at him. Although it was a complete contradiction of what she had always felt, in one burden-shedding, confidence-boosting, heart-soaring moment she recognised the truth of her youthful innocence and ceased to feel ashamed.

'Me, too,' Sorcha said, and for a long, warm, sharing moment they smiled at each other. 'Jorge used to hate it whenever I mentioned a boy-friend,' she said, her mind trawling back over the past, 'so I mentioned lots. Most of them fictitious.'

'You've not dated half the male population of Great Britain?' he protested drolly. 'Yet another illusion bites the dust.'

She laughed. 'I've done my share of love 'em and leave 'em, but I've only had one serious relationship.'

'You've only been intimate with one man?' Rui enquired, and she nodded. 'What was he like?'

'Slim, fair-haired, the same age as me. And a virgin, like me,' Sorcha added.

'So not particularly adept in bed?'

She pulled a face. 'He made love as though he were following an instruction manual.'

'Which is a contributing factor in why you never managed to unlock that mental chastity belt,' Rui declared.

'Could be,' Sorcha acknowledged slowly.

'*Is*,' he insisted. 'Did you love him?'

'No. I told myself I did at the time, but now I think the only reason I had the affair was because I was trying to prove that being molested had not irreparably harmed me.'

He drank the last inch of his wine. 'And now I understand why your stepfather left you your shares—and why you don't want them.'

'I should have decided to sell right at the start,' Sorcha said ruefully, 'but I was busy with my exhibition and I suppose I'd become so used to blocking Jorge from my mind that when I should have thought about him—about the shares and his reason for leaving them to me—I took the easy way out and didn't.' She looked at him. 'Although you're grateful for the way he allowed you to improve Club Marim, you didn't like him much, did you?'

'No. The guy might have been a charmer, yet I always felt he had the eyes of an assassin. And the more he talked about you and revealed more about himself, the less I respected him. Are you tired?' Rui asked when she suddenly yawned.

'I feel worn out. The sun and the wine must have caught up with me.'

'Reliving the past will have been emotionally draining, too,' he said sympathetically. He rose to his feet. 'I'll leave and let you have a nap.'

'What about lunch?' Sorcha protested.

'I'll get something in the coffee shop and you can eat the stuff in the fridge, as and when.'

'I assume you'll be completing your day off by going back to work this afternoon?' she enquired pertly.

Rui grinned. 'Your assumption is incorrect. I intend to have a swim and maybe see if I can persuade Antonio to play squash.' He bent to kiss her on the brow. 'Ciao.'

Sorcha was soon in bed and fast asleep. It was early evening before she awoke. Would Rui return and take her down to the restaurant for dinner? she wondered. For a long time she waited, expecting to hear the jeep at any minute, but finally she filled a plate with salad. He must have called in earlier, she mused as she ate, found her still asleep, and decided to leave her alone for the night. This was a shame—but there was always tomorrow.

## CHAPTER NINE

THE next morning Sorcha started on a water-colour of the hazy purple mountains which rose up in the distance to the north of the cottage. She spent the day painting at her easel—and waiting for Rui. He did not appear. Maybe he felt her disclosure had been so wearing that she needed time and peace in which to recover? She painted at the cottage all day on Sunday, too—if she went out she might miss him—but again he failed to arrive. It was the weekend, Sorcha reminded herself, and after taking Friday off perhaps he had decided to follow through by steering clear of work for a further two days. She could not begrudge him two days. Yet did he need to steer clear of *her*?

Rui would come on Monday. Expecting him to show up in the morning had been unrealistic, Sorcha argued when it reached lunchtime and she remained alone. After a three-day absence from the helm of Club Marim he would have a backlog of matters to clear. Minute by snail-like minute the afternoon trudged by until, impatient with herself and growing increasingly exasperated with him, Sorcha decided to walk down to the hotel.

The water-colour bored her—it fell short of her usual standard anyway—and she had some more postcards which needed to be mailed.

Should she pop her head around Rui's door and say hello? Sorcha wondered as she walked into the lobby. His jeep was parked outside, so presumably he was in his office. She dithered. But he might have someone with him. Or he could be in the middle of dictation. Or on the telephone. Or. Or. Thrusting the cards into the box, she swivelled on her heel and marched out. She was not going to chase him up, dammit. He must come to her.

When Wednesday came around Sorcha decided it was time she received a report on the progress Rui was making in amassing the money to buy her shares. It seemed reasonable that she should be told. Her enquiry was legitimate. Besides, all she would do was ask if everything was proceeding smoothly, listen to the answer, and depart. There would be no complaints about being abandoned. She refused to berate him for his failure to get in touch. She would not advise that, if he had felt cut when she had steered clear of him, she now felt *lacerated*.

She marched down the hill, into the hotel, along the corridor. Reaching his door, Sorcha paused to take a fortifying breath, then she knocked and entered. Rui was reading some papers at his desk, but when he saw her he abandoned them and came forward to greet her.

'Hi,' he said with a grin.

'Good afternoon,' she replied, determined to be businesslike.

She held out her hand in readiness for the usual handshake but, to her confusion, he clasped her waist and drew her to him. Fleetingly his eyes went to her mouth, then he appeared to think again and kissed her on both cheeks instead. Relief swept through her. Joy bubbled. Rui might have stayed away, but his kisses and his desire to hold her close said he still cared.

'I've been wondering how you are,' he said as she sat down opposite him across the desk.

Sorcha shone a dazzling smile. 'I'm busy. Busy painting the mountains. They seem to be full of mystery, even in the sunshine. I've been trying to make them look mysterious in my water-colour, though whether anyone'll realise it is debatable. Mystery is very much in the eye of the beholder,' she said, and stopped, her colour deepening as she became aware of the inanities which had been tumbling out of her. She sat straighter. 'I've come to ask how things are going with regard to the purchase of my shares.'

'Very well,' Rui said. 'In fact, I can guarantee that the cheque will be in your possession before you leave.'

*Before you leave.* The phrase was casual and spoke of acceptance. Didn't he mind that she was due to depart in ten days' time? Wasn't he bothered that once she had shed her holding she would have no further reason to visit Portugal, and to be with him? Sorcha's joy faded. His manner might be friendly and Rui might still care, yet she had a definite sense of . . . withdrawal.

'I look forward to it,' she told him, then gave thanks as the telephone on his desk suddenly shrilled. She was desperate to go and now she had an excuse. 'I'm disturbing you,' she said, rising from her chair. 'I'll speak to you another time. Bye.'

Sorcha returned to the cottage, assembled her beach gear and went down to the beach. Rui still liked her, she thought as she sat on the sand with her arms wrapped around her knees, but he was no longer in the market of loving her—as he had been before. Disconsolately she stared out to sea. Before they had been poised on the brink of what could have been a close and committed relationship, but now when she returned to England he would be grateful.

An oil tanker ponderously edged its way across the horizon. When she had told him of the assault she had suffered there was no doubt she had grabbed Rui's sympathy vote. He had also been adamant that in no way was she to blame. *And* he had seemed convinced that her past

sexual frigidity was not a problem. Yet his
feelings towards her had altered. She was surprised—though she did not know why, Sorcha
brooded unhappily. When she had worked at the
gymnasium hadn't there been a discussion about
an actress who had publicly confessed to being
molested as a child, and hadn't a couple of the
men said that if they came across such a female
they would keep their distance? Be the victim of
abuse and, for some people, you were tainted.
Irrevocably. For all time. Tears burned at the
back of her eyes. Thanks, Jorge, she thought,
swallowing hard. Thank you for bringing Rui and
me together—and for tearing us apart.

The oil tanker disappeared from sight. Yet,
even if their relationship was a lost cause, she
could not regret speaking out. If Rui's attitude
had altered, so had hers—for the better. When
her stepfather had made his assault something
inside her had seemed to die, but it had come
alive again. Her confession had been a turning-
point. She felt cleansed, and stronger. Sorcha
reached for her suntan cream. Before she had
sought to repress the ghosts of her past, but by
confronting them she had exorcised them or, at
least, tamed them. Now she accepted that,
although she had overcome her ordeal, she could
never escape. It was part of the hand life had
dealt and, like it or not, it was a part of her.

\*    \*    \*

When she returned from playing tennis with the keep-fit girls late the following afternoon, a note had been pushed under the door. As she opened it Sorcha's heart raced. Had Rui changed his views? Was this a message suggesting they meet? But the note came from Izabel. On the spur of the moment her parents had decided to celebrate her birthday and engagement to Arnaldo with a dinner party. It was to be held on Saturday at their home in Lagos. Would Sorcha come?

'I'd love to,' she said when she called in to her office the next day. She hesitated. 'Will Rui be going?'

'Naturally.'

Sorcha gave a careful smile. His presence had seemed likely, but she had already decided it did not constitute a reason for her to refuse the invitation. She liked Izabel and she liked meeting new people. Besides, on seeing him, she was not going to fling herself at his feet and plead for understanding, nor give him a hearty kick in the shins and announce that he was prejudiced, small-minded and lacking in all sense of proportion. Though a kick would be satisfying.

'Rui's out at the moment,' Izabel went on, 'but he asked me to say he'll pick you up from the cottage at seven-thirty.'

Common sense might have argued against it, yet when Sorcha opened the door on Saturday it was with the hope, the wish, the fervent prayer that Rui had had second thoughts. Her hopes, wishes and prayers were in vain. He smiled and was amiable. He commented on how her white strapless dress complemented her tan, and his eyes lingered on the honeyed skin of her shoulders. Again he kissed her on both cheeks. But, again, she was aware of his holding back.

Izabel's father was a dentist, and the family lived in a rambling old house which incorporated his surgery, close to the centre of the town. The plain, somewhat drab appearance of the outside belied the interior, which was decorated in elegantly pale colours and furnished with rich, dark furniture. When they arrived they were welcomed with much friendliness. Sorcha's gift for the engaged couple was a pair of embroidered bath towels, while Rui had given them a food mixer. Izabel and Arnaldo—who turned out to be a round-faced, stocky, moustachioed young man—declared themselves delighted.

Next there was Izabel's ring to admire, her parents to meet, introductions to be made. Rui already knew several of the guests, but Izabel insisted on taking Sorcha around to meet each one. A long time ago, when she had been eager to impress her brand-new stepfather, she had learned some Portuguese phrases, and, because returning greetings in her hostess's language had seemed polite, she had swotted them up again. Sorcha was pleased she had, for her efforts were

clearly appreciated, and even her mispronuncia-
tions caused laughter and helped break the ice.
By the time Izabel returned her to Rui she felt at
ease in the gathering.

'*Come, come,*' insisted Izabel's mother, a
bustling, plump woman, steering them through
an archway into the dining-room.

A sumptuous buffet of grilled sardines, stews
and savoury rice awaited, to be followed in due
course by desserts of sticky almond cake and
fresh fruit salad. The wines came from a local
vineyard, and at the end of the meal Portuguese
liqueurs were served, followed by cups of rich
dark coffee.

For the next couple of hours they ate and drank
and chatted, sometimes with Izabel and her
fiancé, and sometimes with their fellow guests,
most of whom could speak reasonable English.

'*Meu amigo*!' exclaimed a boisterous, bearded
man, suddenly bounding through the crowd to
place an arm around Rui's shoulders. '*Como
esta*?'

He replied in Portuguese, then introduced
Sorcha in English. For a while the conversation
continued that way, but eventually the man
lapsed into his mother tongue. Sorcha took the
opportunity to excuse herself. The drawing-room
overlooked a central paved courtyard, where
bougainvillaea climbed in white and purple confusion, and she walked through the open doors

and into the balmy night. Outside several groups were chatting and would have happily included her, but instead she made her way over to a bench in the shadows. After an evening of standing beside Rui, laughing with him, being forever heart-pulsingly *aware* of him, she needed time away. Time to work on her increasingly shaky composure and time to reflect on a decision she had made—almost.

'It is good to get some fresh air,' a soft voice said, and Sorcha looked up to find Izabel beside her. 'I do not think this will be the only engagement party you attend,' she continued.

'Pardon me?'

The Portuguese girl sat down. 'I have been noticing you and Rui, and I think you are in love with each other.'

'No, no,' Sorcha said hurriedly.

'It is no use to protest,' Izabel said, her eyes shining. 'You are in love with him *muito*. And I am in love with Arnaldo *muito*,' she declared, smiling at her fiancé who was approaching across the courtyard with a teenage boy in tow.

The boy, who was one of Arnaldo's cousins, planned to take a cycling holiday in southern England and had come to ask if Sorcha could tell him some good places to visit. Her suggestions were received with much interest and many questions, and meant she was occupied until the party began to break up.

'I have an apology to make,' Rui said soberly when they were driving back to the cottage.

Sorcha's heart leapt. 'Yes?'

'I was wrong about the bus. Ever since we started running the service people have been stopping me to say what a good idea it is.' He turned to smile. 'Thanks.'

'Glad to help,' she said lightly.

After that they fell silent. Rui concentrated on driving through the dark, narrow lanes, while Sorcha was deep in thought.

'Would you like to come in for a coffee?' she said as the jeep came to a halt outside the cottage. 'I know it's after midnight, but I need to talk about something and——'

He smiled. 'A coffee sounds great.'

Sorcha made two mugs and carried them through to the living-room. Rui had opened the double doors and was standing, with his legs apart and his hands in his trouser pockets, gazing out at the night. A warm breeze rippled the surface of the water in the pool and, high above, silver stars twinkled in the black velvet of the sky. As she placed their coffees on a low table in front of the sofa he turned and came to sit beside her.

'I know I'm fouling things up again,' Sorcha said apologetically, 'and I realise it's very late in the day to be changing my mind, and that it'll cause you all kinds of hassle, but——' she gulped in a breath '—I've decided to keep my stake in Club Marim.'

Her nerves tight as piano wire, she waited. What was Rui going to do—fling up his arms in exasperation, declare she ought to be throttled, loudly and angrily *explode*? If so, she could not blame him. But all he did was frown.

'Why?' he asked.

'There are two reasons. The first is Jorge. You said that in deciding to get rid of my shares and dispose of the money I was being contrary. I wasn't. Instead I believed I'd be cutting myself free—of him and of having been abused—but it doesn't work that way. What happened is woven into my life and will always be there,' she said, and went on to explain how, through telling him about the past, her thinking had changed. 'Although this might sound like a cliché,' Sorcha finished at length, 'talking about it to you was character-building. Now I can rise above what happened and take my dividends, enjoy being a part-owner of Club Marim—and occasionally look up to heaven, or down to hell,' she commented succinctly, 'and say "thanks very much, Jorge, you thoroughgoing swine"!'

Rui smiled. 'Attagirl.'

'You aren't annoyed that I'm not selling you my shares?' she asked cautiously.

'No.'

'But you're disappointed?'

'No,' he said again.

Sorcha gave a relieved smile. 'Good, because the second reason for keeping them is you.' She sat back in the corner of the sofa and faced him. 'I realise what Jorge did has tarnished me for you,' she said quickly, 'but——'

'But what?' Rui enquired as her voice petered out and she flushed.

She moistened lips gone dry. Although she had more or less decided she wanted to retain her holding, Izabel's comment about her loving Rui *muito* had forced her to acknowledge how deeply she cared. She did love him, with all her heart and soul. In the jeep Sorcha had decided that, although their relationship seemed to be doomed, if he was worth loving then he must be worth fighting for—even though it might mean the abandonment of every last scrap of her pride. So she had decided to summon up her courage and put herself on the line. And if she was rejected—well, at least she would have given it her best shot.

'But in time maybe you could learn not to mind, as I have,' she continued. 'I mean, it happened more than ten years ago. OK, you think it's a big deal and perhaps you always will, but me keeping my shares also means we'll need to meet from time to time. I want us to meet. I want us to keep in touch. I care for you and——' She saw he was frowning. 'You're thinking that there could be difficulties on—on the sexual side?' she queried hesitantly.

He shook a firm head. 'I've told you before I have absolutely no fears on that score.'

'Oh.' There was a pause. 'I shan't throw myself at you,' Sorcha yattered, 'and, if you decide you could—er—like me, I wouldn't cling.'

'You proposed to me once; are you working up to proposing to me again?' Rui demanded.

Her cheeks flamed. She had not intended to go anywhere near *that* far. Indeed, telling him how important he was to her had been torture enough.

'Er—no.'

'Why not? Are you frightened of being turned down flat a second time?'

Sorcha frowned. There was a glint in his eye which said he could be teasing and deliberately stringing her along...but perhaps she was mistaken?

'Er——' she said again.

Rui's mouth suddenly dimpled at the corners, and he laughed. 'OK, I'll do it.' Moving along the sofa, he interlaced his fingers with hers. 'Please will you be my wife? I don't know how I've progressed from "hello" to "I want us to spend the rest of our lives together" so damn quickly, but I have,' he said as she stared at him. 'And, as for clinging, I'll cling like hell. Marrying me isn't a fate worse than death,' he chided when she continued to gaze in stunned silence.

'But—but ever since I told you about Jorge you've stayed away from me,' Sorcha protested.

'Yes, though not because I considered you were tarnished. Sorcha, I don't,' he insisted. 'I stayed away because I'd decided that the next time we came together—*if* we came together—it must be you who took the lead.'

Her brow puckered. 'Why? I don't understand.'

'It was obvious that talking frankly about the past had left you with a number of things which needed to be sorted out, things it was important you sorted out on your own. And it seemed to me that the only way I could be certain you *had* sorted everything out was to leave you to approach me.' Rui smiled. 'Though what you've just said about accepting the past has proved it anyway.' He put his arm around her shoulders. 'Remember my parents celebrated their fiftieth wedding anniversary? I've always been conscious of their sharing a great love and it made me determined not to marry until I met a woman I couldn't live without.' He drew her close. 'I can't live without you. So—will you marry me?'

'Yes, please,' Sorcha said, and grinned. 'You realise I'm only accepting in order to keep you from leaping off a high cliff?'

'Why else?' he said, straight-faced.

She wrinkled her nose. 'Well, I suppose there's the fact that you're gorgeous and incredibly desirable and—how do you say I love you in Portuguese?' she asked.

'*Eu amo-te.*'

Sorcha smiled into his eyes. '*Eu amo-te.*'

'I love you, too,' Rui murmured, and his mouth possessed hers.

His lips were warm, trembling slightly with the depth of his emotion. She wound her arms around his neck and the kiss deepened, and as his tongue stroked moistly against hers her blood picked up a giddy rhythm. Sorcha moved closer and, from the quickening of his breathing, knew that the push of her breasts against his chest excited him as much as it did her.

'How do you say "please would you make love to me, *now*?"' she enquired.

Rui looked down at her, his eyes dark with passion. 'You don't. Sorcha, you'll never need to ask,' he said huskily, and, taking hold of her hand, he drew her from the sofa and with him through to the bedroom.

'I want to undress you,' he murmured when they were standing in the muted glow of the bedside light. 'I want to reveal your body, inch by delicious inch,' he said, and, reaching behind her, he drew down the long back zip.

Her dress slithered to the floor, leaving her in a strapless white lace bra and pair of tiny lacy briefs. Releasing the catch of her bra, Rui gazed hungrily at her burgeoning breasts and then covered them with his hands. Now it was Sorcha who trembled. His fingers caressed, adored, circled on her nipples until all trembling ceased and she was kissing him, fiercely and hungrily.

He pulled back. 'My beautiful wanton girl,' he said, smiling at her.

Sliding his hands down her, he hooked his thumbs into the fine side-straps of her briefs and eased them from her hips and down. As the shred of lace reached her ankles she stepped out and kicked it aside.

Rui's eyes moved down her. 'Your body's made for love,' he murmured, and reached to brush his fingers across the triangle of tight blonde curls which had been exposed.

Sorcha shuddered, aware of a throbbing hunger. She wanted him to touch her there again—please, *now*—but instead he placed his hands on her waist.

'Now you undress me,' he said.

Momentarily startled by the command, she obediently unfastened his shirt and pushed it from his shoulders, then, with increasing confidence, unbuckled the belt of his trousers. Looking levelly into his eyes, Sorcha took hold of the metal tag of his zip and drew it down.

As his maleness sprung into her hands Rui groaned, and, impatient now, he divested himself of the remainder of his clothes and pulled her on to the bed. Cupping her buttocks, he pulled her urgently against him and began to kiss her with open-mouthed kisses. And, as he kissed her, his hands stroked over her as though her body was a provocative silken mystery which he was determined to solve.

Heat warmed her skin. A restlessness took hold. Lost in an erotic fog, Sorcha felt as though her bones had melted and her body was turning to liquid. She wanted to touch him—needed to touch—and slowly she trailed her fingers down from his shoulders, to the flat plane of his stomach, to his thighs.

For a few minutes he submitted to the pleasure she was giving him but then, murmuring that he could take it no longer, he eased back. Lowering his dark head, he began to skim feather-light kisses over her breasts and down her body until he reached the inner curve of her thigh. Desire gripped, convulsed, and with a gasp she arched against him. An ache, which seemed like an exquisite torture, was growing between her thighs. Relentlessly. Overwhelmingly. Torridly. Rui replaced his mouth with his hand, and as his fingers probed her musky sweetness she instinctively arched against him again.

'Please,' Sorcha said with a husky note of entreaty.

He straddled her and she felt the first push of his male flesh inside her. Her mouth softly bruised from his kisses, her silver-gold hair tumbled around her shoulders, her eyes heavy with love, she looked at him.

'I never realised it could be so good,' she breathed.

Rui smiled. 'It's going to get even better. I promise,' he said throatily.

He thrust deeper, and she felt her body swelling, ripening, enclosing him. Her legs wrapped around his back, Sorcha abandoned herself to the driving rhythm and the fierce accompanying pleasure. Higher and harder, Rui urged her, unleashing all her suppressed longings and taking her to a place of stark sensuality where she had never been before. Desperately she clung, her fingers clutching his back and her nails marking his skin.

Abruptly the rhythm stopped and he was still. Opening her eyes, Sorcha saw he was looking down at her. She smiled and slid her hands down his back to his hips.

'Now,' she gasped, drawing him close.

Rui moved and, in final surrender, she rose up to meet him. Like two waves, they fused, surged, spilled—and became as one.

'When I talked about us getting into bed together it wasn't an expression I'd ever used before,' Rui reflected, some time later. 'But now I know it was wishful thinking.'

'And now I know what it feels like to be well-loved,' Sorcha sighed.

'Takes two,' he murmured.

'The right two.'

He nibbled at her shoulder. 'The perfect two.'

'Mmm,' she agreed dreamily. 'Are you intending to spend the night here?' she asked when he continued to lie there with his arm around her.

Rui gave the contented smile of a man whose life had slotted nicely into place. 'You betcha,' he said.

'But if one of the staff sees your jeep parked outside first thing in the morning, they'll realise——'

'They can realise whatever they like,' he cut in robustly, then he frowned. 'Some time soon we'll need to introduce you as Senhor Almeida's step-daughter and a Club Marim director.'

'And the future Mrs de Braganca.'

He kissed the tip of her nose. 'Especially that.'

'I want to do something,' Sorcha began earnestly. 'I want——'

'To make love again?'

'No.'

Rui drew the lightest of circles around her nipples with his index finger. 'No?' he queried, his mouth slowly curving as the rosy peaks puckered and tightened.

'Yes—in a minute,' she said. 'But what I also want to do is give you two of my shares.'

He shook his head. 'You were left the larger stake and I'm perfectly happy for you to——'

'You're refusing a wedding present from your bride?' Sorcha demanded.

He looked at her and sighed. 'Well, if you put it that way——'

'I do. This doesn't mean I don't intend to be involved with and make my contribution to Club Marim, because I do,' Sorcha went on earnestly. 'I still reckon a shop would be an excellent idea and I know where it could be located. There's a large store-room at the rear of the coffee shop that could easily be——'

Rui drew her close and kissed her. 'You'll need to leave it for later,' he said, 'because the sixty seconds are up.'

# HARLEQUIN PRESENTS®

Don't be late for the wedding!

Be sure to make a date for the happy event—

The first in our tantalizing new selection of stories...

*Wedlocked!*
Bonded in matrimony, torn by desire...

Next month, watch for:
*A Bride for the Taking* by Sandra Marton
Harlequin Presents #1751

Dorian had a problem, and there was only one solution: she had to become Jake Prince's wife! Jake was all too willing to make love to her, but they both knew their marriage was a sham. The trouble was, Dorian soon realized she wanted more, much more, than a few nights of bliss in his arms and a pretense of love—she wanted that pretense to become reality....

Available in July wherever Harlequin books are sold.

# Take 4 bestselling love stories FREE

## Plus get a FREE surprise gift!

## Special Limited-time Offer

**Mail to Harlequin Reader Service®**

3010 Walden Avenue
P.O. Box 1867
Buffalo, N.Y. 14269-1867

**YES!** Please send me 4 free Harlequin Presents® novels and my free surprise gift. Then send me 6 brand-new novels every month, which I will receive months before they appear in bookstores. Bill me at the low price of $2.44 each plus 25¢ delivery and applicable sales tax, if any*. That's the complete price and a savings of over 10% off the cover prices—quite a bargain! I understand that accepting the books and gift places me under no obligation ever to buy any books. I can always return a shipment and cancel at any time. Even if I never buy another book from Harlequin, the 4 free books and the surprise gift are mine to keep forever.

106 BPA ANRH

| | | |
|---|---|---|
| Name | (PLEASE PRINT) | |
| Address | Apt. No. | |
| City | State | Zip |

# HARLEQUIN®

## PRESENTS Plus

**Presents Plus—the power of passion!**

**Coming next month:**

*Edge of Deception* by Daphne Clair
Harlequin Presents Plus #1749

Tara's ex-husband was getting married—but, five years
after their bitter parting, it finally dawned on Tara that
she still loved him! She knew it was a hopeless love.
Their past had been shadowed by an edge of deception,
and neither could forget that he'd accused Tara of an
unforgivable sin....

**and**

*Enemy Within* by Amanda Browning
Harlequin Presents Plus #1750

Ryan Douglas was simply the wrong man for Michaela!
His reputation as a womanizer was legendary, and he
was convinced Mickey had encouraged her half sister
to run off with his wealthy nephew. Now Ryan was
determined to find the missing pair—and insisted
Michaela join him!

**Harlequin Presents Plus**
**The best has just gotten better!**

**Available in July wherever Harlequin books are sold.**

## Announcing
## the New Pages & Privileges™ Program
### from Harlequin® and Silhouette®

### Get All This FREE
### With Just One Proof-of-Purchase!

- **FREE Travel Service** with the guaranteed lowest available airfares plus 5% cash back on every ticket

- **FREE Hotel Discounts** of up to 60% off at leading hotels in the U.S., Canada and Europe

- **FREE Petite Parfumerie** collection (a $50 Retail value)

- **FREE $25 Travel Voucher** to use on any ticket on any airline booked through our Travel Service

- **FREE Insider Tips Letter** full of fascinating information and hot sneak previews of upcoming books

- **FREE Mystery Gift** (if you enroll before June 15/95)

And there are more great gifts and benefits to come! Enroll today and become Privileged!

(see insert for details)

 **PROOF-OF-PURCHASE**

Offer expires October 31, 1996                    HP-PP2